Ruby Parker

SHOOTING STAR

ROWAN COLEMAN

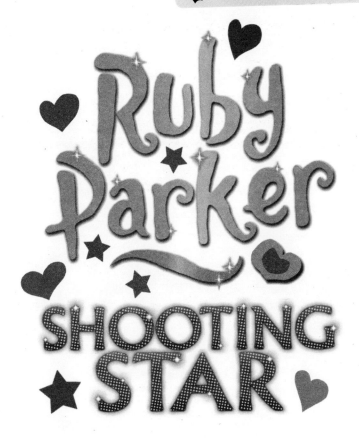

HarperCollins *Children's Books*

First published in Great Britain by HarperCollins *Children's Books* 2009
HarperCollins *Children's Books* is a division of HarperCollins*Publishers* Ltd
77-85 Fulham Palace Road, Hammersmith, London W6 8JB

www.harpercollins.co.uk

1

ISBN 978-0-00-725812-3

Printed and bound in England by
Clays Ltd, St Ives plc

Ruby Parker

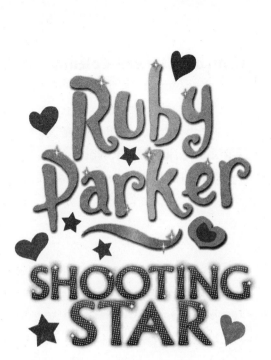

SHOOTING STAR

Also by Rowan Coleman

Ruby Parker: Soap Star
Ruby Parker: Film Star
Ruby Parker: Hollywood Star
Ruby Parker: Musical Star

HIYA! BYE-A! SPOTLIGHT

on Young British Talent

Who can forget the brilliant reality show talent contest *Spotlight!: Search for a Star*? It had us all glued to our seats, right until the brilliant one-off TV special of *Spotlight! The Musical* featuring the best of new young British talent.

The bad news is that the musical's writer – rock legend Mick Caruso – has no plans for another series, telling us at *Hiya! Bye-a!* it was only ever meant to be a one-off. We wonder if that's true or if it has something to do with the surprise last-minute withdrawal of his daughter Jade from the line-up, along with teen heart-throb Danny Harvey.

The good news is that the live broadcast was *so* successful that it's about to be turned into a blockbuster Hollywood musical! Casting is due to start any minute and rumour has it that the stars of the TV special, including Nydia Assimin, Ruby Parker and newcomer Gabe Martinez, are high on the list of preferred actors to win roles. We've also heard that sixteen-year-old international superstar Sean Rivers, who retired recently much to the misery of his global army of fans, might well be up for one of the lead roles in the movie!

Will we see Jade Caruso try out for the lead part of Arial again? It seems unlikely, especially as Mick Caruso told *Hiya! Bye-a!* that he's letting Hollywood get on with it while he concentrates on writing material for his new album, due out next year. And we don't think Hollywood would want to risk big bucks on an unreliable unknown with no track record.

So who will win a part in the biggest teen musical role in Hollywood? Keep your fingers crossed for the Brits and watch this space!

Chapter One

"This is going to be *mega*," Nydia said as I watched her jam clothes into her suitcase. It was the night before all of us – me, Nydia, Anne-Marie, Gabe and Sean – were due to fly out to America to do our screen tests for the movie version of *Spotlight!* Nydia was so excited that she hadn't stopped talking since I arrived to help her choose what to pack, not even to take a breath. "It's so exciting, all of us in America, all of us going to Hollywood! We can go and look at the big sign and stroll along the Walk of Fame. I know you've been before, but this time it'll be better because we'll be with you. It will be *so* exciting that I almost don't even feel nervous about the audition!"

"This is more than an audition," I reminded her as she finally paused for breath. "It's a screen test. To see if we look right, more than anything, and if we do then they'll audition us."

"I know!" Nydia exclaimed, holding up a red and

white print sundress for my approval. "It's going to be the best summer holidays ever!"

I wasn't feeling quite as excited about going to Hollywood as Nydia, Anne-Marie and the rest were. And I wasn't the only one. Sean felt just as nervous about it as I did, probably even more so – with very good reason.

As for me – well, my first Hollywood experience had been a disaster. I had got a part in this film called *The Lost Treasure of King Arthur.* When it came out, it got terrible reviews, mainly about me and how awful I was. I ended up getting fired from my guest role on American TV drama *Hollywood High* and running away back to London without telling my mum where I was going. And when I got back, I told everyone that I was never acting or auditioning again. I even left the Sylvia Lighthouse Academy for the Performing Arts and started at a normal school instead. But somehow acting seemed to follow me around and before I knew it I was part of the chorus in the TV production of Mick Caruso's new musical *Spotlight!* and I had enjoyed it. I realised how much I missed acting, dancing and, since joining the choir at Highgate Comprehensive, even singing! So when we were asked to go and screen-test for the Hollywood film version of the musical, I decided to go. It wasn't until now, when we were actually about to fly off to America, that I started to feel scared about exactly what that meant. Hollywood hadn't been kind to me the last time I was there. Why should now be any different?

"I've got a feeling we'll all get a part," Nydia said, holding up two pairs of sandals and then, after a moment's thought, throwing them both in her suitcase. "Because they've already seen me, Annie and Gabe in the TV special, and they know your work..."

"That's what I'm afraid of," I said, grimacing, thinking about all of those hideous reviews.

"Rubbish!" Nydia laughed. "*The Lost Treasure of King Arthur* might not have been a box-office hit, but it's been at the top of the DVD charts for months now, so you've got nothing to worry about. And if Sean makes a comeback – well, the only thing is if Sean gets the lead, then that means Gabe will get a smaller part, but I don't think he'd mind that much. He's still not totally sure he wants to be an actor anyway. I think he's more interested in the trip to LA."

Gabe was a boy from the Highgate Comprehensive choir. He's a really good singer, but it had taken us a while to persuade him that he could wear dance clothes and still be cool. He was only ever meant to be in the chorus, like me, but Dakshima (my best friend at Highgate Comp) and I found out that Mick Caruso had been cheating, using a thing called an Auto-tune Miracle Microphone. This made his daughter Jade and my ex-boyfriend Danny sound as if they could sing, when really they couldn't. Gabe and Nydia took over the lead roles and so they both got invited to the auditions. But Gabe still loves football more than singing and, to be honest, he got more excited about the thought of a trial for Arsenal's youth squad.

Sean on the other hand would never do the screen test. I knew he wouldn't because he'd told me and only me. It was our secret.

He'd told me the truth earlier that day. It was the last day of term and I'd been walking out of school with Dakshima, Adele, Gabe and some others when I spotted him waiting for me on the other side of the road, leaning up against a brick wall. At one time it would have taken precisely fifteen seconds for Sean to have been ripped to shreds by the hordes of teenage schoolgirls who were all madly in love with him. But recently the girls of Highgate Comp had got used to the fact that one of their number hung out with former international teen heart-throb Sean Rivers. So nowadays all they did was pretend not to notice him and then giggle hysterically once he was out of sight.

"Hiya," Dakshima said casually, as he fell into step beside us.

"Hey," he said. "What's up?"

"What are you doing here?" I asked him with a smile.

"Well, the Academy broke up yesterday and Anne-Marie's shopping her head off for clothes to take to Hollywood, because apparently the fifteen closets-worth she already has aren't enough, so I thought that maybe you'd like to go get an ice cream with me," Sean said.

"Sounds cool," Dakshima said happily.

"Um, actually," Sean looked sideways at me. "It was really just Ruby I wanted to talk to." He treated Dakshima to one of his sweetest smiles. "It's nothing personal; just some stuff I want to tell her about the trip – totally boring stuff..."

"Ooh, secrets," Dakshima teased him, but with a smile. "What secret could you and Ruby have? I hope Anne-Marie knows or else there'll be trouble..."

"Do I need to come then?" asked Gabe. "Only I can't because I said I'd play footy down the sports centre. Under sixteens five-aside tournament."

"Don't worry," Sean told him. "It's nothing important."

"I'm off then," Gabe said, winking at me. "See you at the airport."

"Hey! Wait for me," Dakshima said. "I might as

well come and watch you if this lot are going to be all film starry."

After they had gone I looked at Sean.

"Just boring stuff?" I asked him. "I've never heard such a lame excuse in my life. What's the real deal?"

"Hollywood," Sean had said. "I've decided that I'm going with you."

"You are?" I was shocked. "I mean, that's great. It'll be a lot of fun to have you on the trip and Anne-Marie will be thrilled. But you seemed so certain that you didn't want to try and get a part in the film. That you were happy with how your life is now."

"I am, but..." Sean began before trailing off as we approached the ice-cream van.

"Has Anne-Marie finally got you to give in?" I asked him. Anne-Marie Chance was one of my best friends, but as funny and kind and as loyal as she could be, she had never really got used to the idea that her boyfriend was the *former* international teen heart-throb Sean Rivers. They had been going out together for nearly a year now and she never tired of telling us over and over again that Sean was wasted, hiding himself away in school in England, and that he should be back out there, taking charge of his career and making the most of his talents. Since Sylvia Lighthouse told Sean that he'd been offered the chance to screen-test for *Spotlight!* too, Anne-Marie had badgered him non-stop in a bid to get him to come to Hollywood with the rest of us.

"It's not Anne-Marie." He paused as he paid the ice-cream man for two ninety-nines.

"Then what is it?" I asked him, puzzled. "Why are you going back?"

Since moving to London, Sean had seemed like such a happy, settled person, not at all like the troubled boy I'd met on the set of *The Lost Treasure of King Arthur.* We had nearly fallen out the last time I went to Hollywood because I'd accidentally given away his secret location to the world press during an interview on national TV, but even then in the end he'd ended up being a really good friend to me. I hadn't seen him look this worried since and that worried me. I realised I cared about Sean a lot.

"It's Dad," Sean said simply, with a shrug.

"Your dad?" I asked him with surprise. "Has he been trying to bully you, Sean? Because if he has you have to tell someone."

Sean had lived with his dad after his parents split up, because his dad had told Sean that his mum didn't want him any more. Pat Rivers had kept Sean and his mum apart for years. While filming *The Lost Treasure of King*

Arthur I'd realised exactly how cruelly Sean's dad treated him, making him work all year round and sometimes even hitting him. It was because of Pat Rivers that Sean had decided that the world would never see his amazing acting talent ever again. He'd had enough of celebrity life.

That was why his answer was so confusing. How could the man who drove him out of show business get him to go back to it?"

"No, he hasn't been in touch," Sean said with a shrug. "And in a way that's why I want to go to Hollywood."

I was so surprised by what he said that I'd forgotten to eat the ice cream and now it was dribbling down my elbow. I licked my wrist as I waited for him to continue.

"I haven't seen Dad in nearly a year," Sean said, studying his trainers as we sat down on the grass. "At first he tried to contact me, but Mum returned all of his letters and stopped his calls. And for a long time that was the way I wanted it, but now..."

"You've changed your mind?" I asked in amazement. "After everything he did?"

"He's my dad, Ruby," Sean said. "Yes, he was a terrible dad, but he's the only one I have. I thought that maybe now he doesn't have my career to obsess over, he might have changed. I've been wondering if we can make up."

"And the only way you can think of to make that

happen is to go back to being in films again?" I asked. "Because you know, Sean, if you go up for the lead in *Spotlight!* you will get it. No one else will stand a chance. And before you know it you'll be walking the red carpet and dodging the paparazzi again, and if you get back together with your dad... well, have you forgotten how hard he made your life?"

Sean shook his head. "That's the point. I don't want my life to go back to how it was. I don't want a part in *Spotlight!* I don't want any of that. All I want is the chance to see my dad and talk to him. And my dad's in Hollywood. But I told Mom I'd screen-test and see how it goes."

"And she thought that was a good idea?" I asked.

"She said if it's what I really want then she'll support me," Sean said, not meeting my gaze.

"But it's *not* what you really want, is it?" I said, trying hard to understand. "Why don't you just tell her that you want to see your dad? I'm sure she'd be fine with it, help you make the arrangements and everything."

"No... I can't," Sean said quickly. "The last time Dad was around, Mom ran away. I didn't see her for years and years. The only reason she found me again was because of you. It's not like your parents, Ruby. Even though they've split up they still like each other, care about each other even. Mine *hate* each other. My mom doesn't want me to have anything to do with Dad ever again. And I thought I felt that way too, for a while."

"And now you don't?"

"Now I don't know how I feel," Sean said. "But I know Mom would never let me see Dad. The only way I'm going to get the chance to see if he's changed is if I go to Hollywood and pretend that I want to audition for that part."

"And try and see your dad in secret?" He nodded.

"But what are you going to do when they offer you the part?" I asked. "It'll be the biggest news in Hollywood since – well, since you quit acting."

"I'll worry about that if it happens," Sean said, smiling at me, but with none of the usual sparkle. "Right now I have to figure out a way to see my dad once we get there."

"I can't help feeling that your plan is nearly as bad as my plan to run away from Hollywood to London in the middle of the night," I told him.

"Maybe, but it's the only plan I've got," Sean said ruefully.

"Have you told Anne-Marie?" I tried to imagine what my friend would think about his crazy scheme.

"Nope," Sean said. "I haven't told anyone but you, Ruby Parker."

"Why me?" I asked, feeling pleased and worried at the same time.

Sean smiled at me, and this time there was a real warmth that was difficult to resist. "Because I know I can trust you. And besides, every hero needs a sidekick, right?"

"Oh, so now I'm your sidekick!" I'd said, unable to stop myself smiling back.

"You bet," Sean said. "And so much more."

I'd walked back from the park and round to Nydia's house feeling confused and worried. I was glad Sean had talked to me, but I had seen how mean his dad was to him. I didn't know if it was a good idea for Sean to try and contact him, especially without his mum knowing. But Sean had trusted me with his secret, me alone, and I knew that as one of his best friends, I would keep that secret and help him in whatever way I could.

But I had the distinct feeling that it wasn't going to be easy.

teen girl! Magazine's

Where has all the talent gone?

We at the TGM! newsdesk can confidently predict that our readers' celeb-spotting photos page will be empty of your snaps this week. Why? Because all of our favourite stars are flying off to Hollywood in the hopes of winning a role in the movie of **Mick Caruso's** hit musical ***Spotlight!***

The brilliant leads for the UK telly hit Nydia Assimin and cute newcomer **Gabe Martinez** will be hoping they get to play Arial and Sebastian again in the film, but they'd better watch out because they are up against some top competition. Making a comeback AT LAST is our favourite former soap star **Ruby Parker**, who will also be hoping to score a role in the film, and even more excitingly TGM! can exclusively reveal that former international teen heart-throb **Sean Rivers** himself has gone with them. We seriously hope that rumour is true because we know that all our TGM! readers would love to see Sean on the big screen again.

Meanwhile, it's official. **Danny Harvey** has left ***Kensington Heights*** for good. He exclusively told TGM! that he's decided he wanted to try something new and exciting, and he's certainly achieved that. TGM! can exclusively reveal that our Danny has landed the part of the young Guy of Gisborne in the new Disney movie ***The Young Robin Hood.*** Danny told TGM! that he's really looking forward to filming this summer and especially to playing a baddy. One thing we at TGM! know is that Danny is going to have to work hard to stay at the tip of our top ten hottest lads poll as the actor playing the title role of Robin Hood is none other than ***Hollywood High*** hunk **Hunter Blake**. Pack a picnic, girls, it looks like Sherwood Forest is going to be the top tourist spot this summer!

Chapter Two

"I can't believe it," Anne-Marie said, whisking the copy of *Teen Girl! Magazine* that I'd bought at the airport out of my hands and staring at the article.

"Can't believe what?" Nydia was sitting between us with her eyes closed. It turned out that Nydia didn't like flying. None of us had known this because until today Nydia hadn't flown anywhere. The minute that the plane's engines had begun to roar in preparation for take-off, she had given a little shriek and closed her eyes. That was about twenty minutes ago.

"I can't believe it either," I said, reaching across Nydia and grabbing the magazine back. "Danny and Hunter *together* on a film? The only two boys I have ever kissed working together all summer! How did that happen?"

"Really?" Nydia opened one eye. "That's massive."

"That's not what I can't believe," Anne-Marie said. "I can't believe they didn't mention my name once. Not *once*! Everyone else was: Nydia, you, Gabe, Sean – but not me. Why not? I'm on this plane too. I got good reviews in *Spotlight!* Why wouldn't they mention me?"

Nydia opened her other eye and looked at me. "Danny and Hunter are working together? How come this is the first we've heard of it?"

"They'll hang out," I said miserably. "They'll be friends. They'll get to like each other and then they'll talk about me. They will discuss me."

"Not a mention," Anne-Marie said, scanning the article again. "Not even a photo."

"That's not true," Nydia said, sitting up and leaning over. "There you are in that one."

"Where?" Anne-Marie scrutinised a photo of me and Nydia, grinning like Cheshire cats at the aftershow party of the TV broadcast.

"Look, that's your elbow, just in the corner there," Nydia said, winking at me.

Anne-Marie scowled. "Ha ha – very funny. Amazing how you can be so funny when we are thirty thousand feet up in the air in barely more than a flying tin can that could crash to the earth at any moment."

Nydia shut her eyes again. "I think I might be sick," she said.

"You've got a point though," I said, shaking my head at Anne-Marie. "Why didn't we know about *The Young*

Robin Hood? After all, if anyone at the Academy gets a part Sylvia Lighthouse tells everyone. It's announced in assembly. And they must have cast it ages ago – soon after Danny dropped out of *Spotlight!* I know he's not talked to me since that party, but he still hangs out with Sean sometimes, doesn't he?"

"No, actually." Anne-Marie glanced a few rows back to where Sean was sitting next to Gabe playing his Nintendo DS. "They haven't hung out for ages. Danny's spent more time with Jade than anyone this term, though they aren't going out together I don't think."

"Maybe there was a confidentiality clause," Nydia said. "Maybe that's why it wasn't announced."

I sighed and looked out of the window at the clouds below. At the aftershow party I'd thought that Danny was on the verge of asking me out again. Even after I told him that basically he was one of the worst singers I had ever heard, and that all the time he thought he had a brilliant voice it was really the Auto-tune Miracle Microphone making him sound good. Even after he had to drop out of the lead role in *Spotlight!* because of me I thought that maybe he still liked me, because I knew that I still liked him. But then we'd been interrupted and he hadn't said anything. And I hadn't heard from him since.

In the last few weeks I'd been busy helping Jeremy

Fort (my mum's boyfriend and legend of film and theatre) find a nice house to buy in London, getting ready to come out to Hollywood and getting on with everyday life at Highgate Comprehensive. I hadn't really had a chance to think about Danny and I'd decided that was a good thing. So now I learn about him and Hunter from a magazine.

"Look," Anne-Marie said, "the least of your worries is whether or not Danny Harvey and Hunter Blake might be scoring your kissing technique out of ten."

"I hadn't thought of that!" I cried, clapping my hands over my eyes.

"I had," Nydia said.

"It doesn't matter anyway because they will be in Sherwood Forest or wherever and you will be in Hollywood. Thousands of miles away. So don't even think about them. Concentrate on the screen tests. If we all get parts in this film we can spend the whole of the summer in America, and it will be so much fun! My mum might even be in LA for a week in August and I haven't seen her since Easter, so she's bound to let me go shopping with her credit card. And once Sean takes the part of Sebastian the whole town will be after him again. All the paparazzi wanting to shoot his picture, C! the Celebrity Channel will want to interview him, and everyone will be wondering – who is that mysterious yet glamorous blonde girl with him? *Me,* that's who it will be, and then *I* will be on TV and in every magazine, and *Teen Girl! Mag* can go and take a running jump." Anne-Marie clapped her hands together. "It's going to be so exciting!"

If only she knew what I knew she wouldn't be so happy. I felt a knot in my tummy and looked out of the window. Maybe Anne-Marie was right. Maybe I should stop thinking about Danny and Hunter getting to know each other in Sherwood Forest. They were thousands of miles away and there was nothing I do about it. I just had to put it out of my mind. What I couldn't forget so easily was that in order to keep my promise to one best friend, I had to lie to another. It was a difficult place to be.

Mum and I had helped Jeremy find a nice house in Highgate, not too far away from our house. But he had decided to keep his house in Beverly Hills after all and I was glad of that because he'd said that we could all stay there while we were in Hollywood. There were three adults and five kids on the trip. Mum was in charge of me, Nydia and Anne-Marie, as Nydia's parents couldn't get time off work and Anne-Marie's mum and dad were working on the other side of the world again. I thought it was a bit much, because even when Anne-Marie was going halfway around the world, she still couldn't seem to catch up with her parents. Sean and his mum were coming, and Gabe and his dad. Jeremy wouldn't be there. He was in a play about seagulls in London, getting rave reviews. But his chef and housekeeper, Augusto and Marie, were and best of all his little dog David, who I had really missed quite a lot, although I would never tell my cat Everest that.

"This place is *huge*!" Nydia exclaimed as our minibus drew up to the front door.

"It's amazing," Anne-Marie said, sliding her sunglasses down her nose so she could get a better look at the house. Back in London Anne-Marie lived, more or less by herself, in one of the biggest, grandest houses I had ever seen, so for her to be impressed by Jeremy's place was pretty unusual.

"All the houses round here are like this," I told her. "This is where all the film stars live."

Looking at Jeremy's house made me feel a bit funny in the pit of my stomach. The last time I was here it was the most unhappy I'd ever been, even more than when Mum and Dad were splitting up, because at least then I knew they loved me. When I ran away from Hollywood,

I didn't think that anyone did. This time would be different I told myself. This time if I didn't enjoy it out here, I knew Mum would take me straight home. And anyway I was different now. I was fourteen and I wasn't a little girl any more.

"Oh my God, what is *that*!" Anne-Marie shrieked as David raced out of the front door and leapt into my arms. I grimaced as he licked me all over my face with his tiny rough tongue.

"This is David," I managed to say. "He's Jeremy's dog. He look likes a rat, but actually once you get to know him he's quite nice."

"He hasn't forgotten you," Augusto said as he walked out to greet us, followed by Marie. "I think he sensed you the minute you got off the plane; he's been waiting by the door for an hour."

"Augusto!" I said, giving him a big hug that nearly squeezed David to death. "And Marie, it's so nice to see you two again!"

"We're very glad to have you and your friends stay with us," Marie said, smiling at everyone. "Especially you, young lady. You gave us such a fright the last time. Come on, I'll show you your rooms and then Augusto and I thought some cool drinks and sandwiches by the pool."

"Woohoo!" Gabe whooped and Nydia laughed as everyone ran off to find which room they would be staying in.

"Coming in, honey?" Sean's mum watched as Sean crouched down on the drive and made a fuss of David, rolling him on his back and tickling his little tummy.

"Be right there," Sean said.

I knelt down next to him as he stroked the dog. "Feeling weird?" I asked.

He nodded, but didn't look at me. "You?"

"Yeah, I am, but I reckon I'll be OK. I'm not on my own this time, am I?"

Sean smiled at me, his blue eyes twinkling. "I'll look out for you," he said.

"So have you worked out how you're going to give your mum the slip, go and find your dad and see if you can work things out with him, all while somehow managing not to get the lead part in a film that would be perfect for you and getting your picture in every single magazine on the whole planet?" I asked him.

Sean shook his head. "Nope. But I'm working on it."

"Well, let me know when you do," I said.

"Don't you worry, Ruby, you will be the first to know," Sean told me, standing up and offering me his hand. Somehow that didn't make me feel any better.

* * *

Half an hour later and all of us kids were in the pool, while the adults sat around it eating some of Augusto's amazing BLTs. David was sitting up on his hind legs and begging for scraps.

"This is the business," Mr Martinez said. "You get yourself a life like this, son, and I'll be happy."

"I will do when I'm playing for Arsenal," Gabe said, winking at Nydia and making her laugh. I noticed that those two had started to spend quite a lot of time together lately.

"We've got an early start tomorrow," Mum said. "We all have to be at the studios at eight, so you all need an early night tonight." Everyone groaned. "I'm serious. No midnight feasts or talking after lights out."

"Mum!" I protested. "We're not babies any more. We don't do midnight feasts."

"Mmm well, good," Mum said. "Come on, you lot. Out and get ready for bed. It's a big day tomorrow and you've had a long day."

Moaning, the five of us pulled ourselves out of the pool and wrapped ourselves in bathrobes.

"You can actually see the Hollywood sign from here," Anne-Marie said, smiling at Sean. "This place is so amazing, aren't you glad that you're back?"

Sean looked, his face expressionless. "I don't know yet," he said.

"Of course you are," Anne-Marie said. "It's going to be great! You'll get the lead in the film and you'll be famous again, and the whole town will love you and me, your girlfriend, and I'll get my big break and nothing will ever be the same." Anne Marie flung her arms around Sean and hugged him.

"We'll see," Sean said, glancing at me over Anne-Marie's shoulder.

"Don't be silly," Anne-Marie said. "When have you ever not got a part that you've gone for?"

"There's always a first time," Sean said.

Later, while the parents were still downstairs, Anne-Marie, Nydia and I lay on my bed with the balcony doors open, letting the warm night air in as we ate a packet of cookies that I had snaffled from the kitchen when no one was looking. I was feeding crumbs to David who had curled up on my feet as if he was really pleased to see me.

"What will it be like tomorrow?" Nydia asked me.

"I don't know," I said. "I haven't done this before either.

Every single audition I've ever been to has been different. I have no idea what they ask you to do at a screen test."

"It doesn't matter anyway," Anne-Marie said. "Because we are prepared, aren't we?"

Nydia and I looked at each other. For the last month Anne-Marie had made us meet at her house three times a week to learn the lines from the play and rehearse all the songs over and over again. "No one knows *Spotlight!* better than us. They'll have to choose us, they'll just *have* to."

"But they might not," I said carefully. I had the feeling that getting a part in the film meant more to Anne-Marie than anyone else. "They might want American kids and I heard that Sunny Dale might be up for Arial."

"She's *rubbish,*" Anne-Marie said. "I can knock spots off her any day of the week, and if they think I'm going to have that girl screen-kissing my boyfriend then they've got another think coming."

"I hadn't thought of that," Nydia said. "If you or me got the lead we might have to kiss Sean too, Ruby. How disgusting would that be!"

"Yuck!" I said, and I pulled a suitable face. But worryingly, the second Nydia mentioned it I realised I didn't think it would be too awful to kiss Sean Rivers at all. I thought of that twinkly, blue-eyed smile he'd given me earlier that day and for the first time since I'd known him it made my tummy lurch. But not in bad way.

"Oh no, that's a terrible, terrible idea!" I said out loud before I realised it. "That would be really, really bad."

"He's not that bad a kisser," Anne-Marie giggled, whacking me with one of my pillows.

"Well, he's been kissing you for nearly a year so he can't be *that* good," I teased her, keen to get the stupid feeling out of my tummy.

"Attack!" Nydia yelled, launching herself at me with the final cushion.

There were feathers all over the floor by the time my mum caught us.

SPOTLIGHT! THE MOVIE MUSICAL

SCREEN TEST SCENE

SCREENPLAY BY JOSETTE HUGHES AND SIMION HUGHES* based on *LYRICS AND MUSIC BY MICK CARUSO* and *BOOK BY DEN FELTON

Scene 37

Ext. Evening. Fire escape at the back of the drama school. ARIAL is sitting on her own, crying. A figure appears at the window. It's SEBASTIAN. He hesitates and then climbs out of the window and sits beside her. He considers putting a hand on her shoulder, but in the end is not brave enough.

SEBASTIAN

Arial, why are you crying?

ARIAL looks up at him, as if she's only just realised that he is there.

Hastily she wipes her tears away and tries to smile.

ARIAL

I'm not crying, I just have… um hay fever. That's all - it makes my eyes run.

SEBASTIAN hesitates again. He knows that ARIAL is lying, but he doesn't want to embarrass her.

SEBASTIAN

Look, I know you haven't got very many friends here yet, and that some of the girls are giving you a hard time - but that's only because they are jealous. Only because you are more talented than they are. Kinder, nicer, funnier and more beautiful…

ARIAL looks up sharply at SEBASTIAN.

ARIAL

Pardon?

SEBASTIAN looks scared and then
his face changes as he makes a decision
to say what he's really thinking.

SEBASTIAN

I said I think you are really beautiful.

They look at each other for a moment
longer and then SEBASTIAN loses
his courage. He climbs back in
through the window, leaving ARIAL
sitting alone once again.

Cue production number four SEBASTIAN
and ARIAL'S 1ST DUET "I'm in Love!"
Sung as a duet but shot in two
separate locations: SEBASTIAN'S
room and the fire escape.

"I'm in Love!"

ARIAL: I've never felt this way before.
I see your face and my heart
hits the floor.

SEB: I don't understand what's going on,
Only that I miss you whenever
you're gone.

BOTH: I feel crazy and happy and sad.
I feel lazy and zappy and mad!
I want to sing, I want to run,
to fly in the sky above!
What's happening to me?
Could it be that I'm in love?

SEB: None of the guys have ever felt
the way I do.

ARIAL: All of the girls would laugh if
they ever knew.

BOTH: But I'd do anything to spend a
few minutes with you
Because only you can make me
feel the way I do.
I feel funny and stupid and fine!
And Honey I wish that Cupid
would make you mine!
I want to sing, I want to run,

to soar in the sky above!
What's happening to me?
Could it be I'm in love?

DANCE INTERLUDE

SEB: None of the guys have ever felt
the way I do.

ARIAL: All of the girls would laugh if
they ever knew.

BOTH: But I'd do anything to spend a
few minutes with you
Because only you can make me
feel the way I do.
I feel funny and stupid and fine!
And Honey I wish that Cupid
would make you mine!
I want to sing, I want to run,
to soar in the sky above!
What's happening to me?
Could it be I'm in love?

Music fades. SEBASTIAN looks wistfully out of his bedroom window at the moon and then draws down his blind as his roommates enter. ARIAL takes one more look at the moon and then climbs back in through the window, pulling it down behind her. Scene closes.

Chapter Three

"Right," I said to everyone as we sat in the waiting room right outside where the screen testing was, with a slight note of panic in my voice. "All we have to do is act, sing and dance. It will be fine."

"It won't be fine," Nydia said anxiously. "This isn't a scene, it's a whole act! I thought they'd give us less to do and more time to prepare. I thought we'd get the scene and then at least have a chance to rehearse. I didn't think they'd hand us a huge script and then tell us we'll be seen on set in about five minutes. And that was four minutes ago!"

"Don't panic," Gabe said, taking her hand. "This is your role. You've played Arial on TV in front of millions. OK, so this is a new song and a new scene that none of us have ever seen before, written especially for the film. But it's still Arial, and you still know how to play Arial better than anyone."

Nydia smiled at him and I thought that I really had to

get her on her own soon and ask exactly what was happening between those two. But now wasn't the time.

"Gabe's right," I said. "We've prepared as much as anyone could. Now we just have to do our best."

"How can you be so calm?" Nydia asked, dropping Gabe's hand as if she'd only just realised that she was holding it.

"By pretending mostly," I said. "Look, if you don't want to do it, just say. Nothing bad will happen, except that you definitely won't get a part in the film and will have to spend the summer in London."

"I want to do it," Nydia said, biting her lip. "Only in about two *weeks*, not two minutes!"

"I really wanted to do my scene with Sean." Anne-Marie spoke for the first time since she'd been handed the script. "We'd be so good together in this scene. I can't believe that he's not here."

That morning Sean had woken up with a temperature and a sore throat. He'd told, or rather croaked to, his mum that he wouldn't be able to screen test-after all. His mum had phoned the studio to tell them and they said they had to go ahead and start the casting process today, but that they'd be happy to wait for Sean to get better before they made the final decision on male roles. By which they meant the part of Sebastian, because there would never be any way that Sean Rivers would get any part in any film that wasn't the lead.

I'd found Sean lying on the sofa watching TV just before we left.

"Well, there are no radiators on in here, it's much too hot," I said, crossing my arms and tipping my head on one side. "So tell me – how did you fake your temperature?"

"Dipped the thermometer in a mug of tea," he confessed in his normal voice. I shook my head. It was hard to be cross with Sean, but I wanted to give it a go.

"OK, so you've managed to get out of it today, but how long are you going to be able to keep it up? You can't have a sore throat forever, you know."

"I know," Sean said, grinning at me. "I was thinking it could progress to a chesty cough, maybe a rash and then, oh, I don't know – the bubonic plague. That would do it."

I tired hard not to laugh, but failed.

"Have you worked out how you are going to reach your dad yet?" I asked, glancing at the door to make sure we weren't being overheard.

"No," Sean admitted. "But I will. The first thing I have to do is find out his address, because he's moved. I need to find out where he is living or working. I'm going to do that today."

"Your mum is staying home with you," I reminded him in a whisper as I heard voices in the hall. "You won't just be able to look him up in *Yellow Pages*."

"I know," Sean said. "I wasn't in the movie *Kid: Super Spy* for nothing, you know. I picked up a few tricks of the trade." He smiled at me again, that same but new smile that suddenly seemed to unsettle me the way it did every other girl in the entire world. I didn't like it.

"Don't smile at me," I said without thinking, as my tummy did a backflip.

"What? Why not?" Sean asked me.

I stared at him for a second or two trying to think of something to say that didn't involve the words "because I think I'm getting a bit of a crush on you for some bizarre reason and you smiling at me only makes it worse".

"I... um... because I am in the zone. If you smile at me I'll want to smile at you and then I'll be out of the, er, zone thingy and um... It's like Anne-Marie, your girlfriend and my best friend, is always saying, you have to stay in the zone."

Sean's smile widened. "You are crazy, Ruby Parker," he told me. "But that's what I've always liked about you."

"Sean!" Anne-Marie rushed into the room wearing a paper mask over her face, presumably to protect her from his germs. "Are you sure you can't come? Because when you get out there in front of the camera, the adrenaline will kick in and I'm sure you'll be fine."

"Can't talk," Sean croaked, shrugging apologetically.

"But I really *want* you to come," Anne-Marie said miserably.

"Break a leg," Sean had managed, and I dragged Anne-Marie out to the car.

And now we were in a room waiting to be called for a screen test. The funny thing was that on the other side of the door was a full-size movie set of a building, complete with a life-size fire escape that each of us was supposed to perform a "dance interlude" on. For the first time ever in my acting career, it was quite likely that I actually would break a leg.

Chapter Four

On the way back to Jeremy's house we were all silent. Finally Anne-Marie spoke up.

"I can't believe how awful I was!" she moaned miserably, staring out of the car window.

"You weren't *that* bad," Gabe told her. "At least you remembered the words. I forgot every other line. I'm sorry, Anne-Marie. I messed up and I know it means a lot more to you than it does to me."

Gabe and Anne-Marie had been paired together for their screen test, whereas Nydia and I had two total strangers as our Sebastians.

"It wasn't your fault," Anne-Marie said, smiling wanly at Gabe. "At least when you said your lines you were brilliant. I remembered all of mine, but I might as well have been reading them off the back of a packet of cornflakes for all the feeling that I managed to get in them. And the song!" She clutched suddenly at her throat. "Maybe I'm catching Sean's sore throat. Maybe that's why my singing was so off."

"At least you two knew each other," said Nydia. "My Sebastian was a metre taller than me and he couldn't look me in the eye. There's nothing more off-putting than a boy telling you he thinks you're beautiful when he's gazing at your left ear."

"You've been very quiet, Ruby," Anne-Marie said. "What was your Sebastian like?"

I had been standing looking up with some trepidation at the fire escape where I was soon to be sitting when I had been introduced to my Sebastian.

"Ruby, isn't it?" A lady with headphones and a clipboard approached me. "You have about twenty minutes before we start filming your scene. Now would be a good time for you to meet Henry Dufault. He'll be your Sebastian today."

She'd stood aside to reveal a boy of about fifteen with a distinct look that wasn't like any other boy I knew. Henry had long dark hair that reached down to his shoulders and fell across his brown eyes, which looked as if they were lined with eyeliner. He wore a red T-shirt featuring a band I was not nearly cool enough to have heard of, skinny black jeans and a pair of bright green cowboy boots. He was not at all how I imagined Sebastian. Or anyone, for that matter.

"Oh, hello," I said, suddenly sounding very English and proper.

"Hey," Henry nodded and smiled.

"Do you want to talk the scene through before we start?" I asked him as the lady with the headphones and clipboard headed off. "Work out any moves or anything?"

Henry raised one amused brow as if he thought the suggestion was a completely silly one. "Let's wing it," he said with a grin. "It'll be a buzz."

"Wing it?" I asked him, sounding a bit squeaky. "A buzz? Do you mean improvise?"

"Winging is always best," Henry told me. "Keeps it fresh, real. Let's just follow each other, cool?"

I'd nodded.

"This is going to be terrible," I'd whispered to myself as I took my seat on the fire escape.

But weirdly enough it wasn't and neither was Henry. He could act as well as any boy I knew, even Sean, and he had a better singing voice than all of them. Even though I couldn't see him when we sang our duet I could sort of feel his voice; it was so strong that it gave me confidence to push my voice further. I had never enjoyed singing a song so much before and I realised that whether I got a part in *Spotlight! The Movie Musical* or not, I had enjoyed my screen test when none of my friends had. And that was why I was quiet.

"So?" Nydia prompted me as the car pulled into Jeremy's driveway. "How did it go?"

"I don't know," I said honestly, looking at my friends. "I think it went OK. But we'll soon find out because if they still want us they will be calling us back tomorrow."

"I just want you to know," Anne Marie said suddenly, grabbing mine and Nydia's hands, "if I don't get called back and you two do there will be no hard feelings at all."

"Yeah, right," me and Nydia said at once, rolling our eyes. All three of us laughed and the tension in the car disappeared in an instant.

"Whatever happens, best friends forever," Nydia said.

"Best friends forever," Anne-Marie and I agreed.

But as we walked into the house I saw Sean watching us from an upstairs window. He was waving a piece of paper at me, grinning exactly like a boy who had just found out what he needed to know.

Over dinner the parents talked and talked about the screen tests, and the other kids they had seen there, and what our chances were of getting called back for a second round of auditions, and whether or not we had a chance of getting any part in the film, never mind the leads. But us kids just ate our food and tried to talk about something else.

"You seem to be much better, Sean," I said, looking across at him. He had been trying to get me on my own since we'd got back and so far I'd managed to avoid him.

I had decided it was no good. I couldn't be Anne-Marie's best friend forever and keep a secret about her boyfriend from her. Worse still, I couldn't be her best friend and start having weird feelings about Sean. The only thing to do was to try and avoid him as much as possible. If he wanted to track his dad down then that was fine, but he'd have to do it without me until these funny feelings went away and Anne-Marie knew about the real reason he'd come to Hollywood. *That* was proper best friend behaviour.

"I'm not sure," Sean said. "I think I'm getting a cough."

After dinner we decided to watch a film in Jeremy's huge screening room. It was a bit like a mini cinema, only it had ten great big comfy chairs that you could swivel round on. We'd been watching the film for about twenty minutes when I went to get us some more microwave popcorn, because we'd eaten the first lot before the film had even started. I was standing in the empty kitchen holding David in my arms, waiting for the microwave to beep, when Sean crept up on me.

"Boo!" he said, chuckling away as if he were hilarious. I was so surprised that I nearly dropped David, who went into a frenzy of barking and general guarding which might have been scary if he had been slightly bigger than a large mouse.

"Sean!" I hissed as I calmed David. "What are you doing here?"

"I've got it," he said, handing me a page he had torn out of the local directory. He'd obviously looked his father up in the *Yellow Pages* after all. "You were right – I didn't need superspy skills to track Dad down. He's here, Pat Rivers Talent Agency. I'm going to go and see him."

"When?" I asked anxiously. I had been hoping that it would take ages for Sean to find his dad. It hadn't occurred to me that it would really be as simple as looking him up in a phone book.

"Tonight," Sean said, watching me intently.

"Tonight? But it's his office address. Even if you could sneak out he won't be there at this hour."

Sean shook his head. "Ruby, you met my dad – when did he ever stop working?"

I thought for a second. "Never."

"Exactly. He's famous for his crazy working hours. Of course he'll be there. He probably *lives* there, knowing Dad."

"Well, if he does then it doesn't sound like he's changed much, does it?" I reminded Sean.

"Maybe not, but if I don't speak to him I won't know." He put a hand on my shoulder. "Anyway I've worked out how we are going to get there."

"*We?*" I squeaked. "As in you and me? I am not coming with you, Sean. It's not fair of you to make me. Anne-Marie's your girlfriend – don't you think you should be inviting *her* on stupid trips across LA in the middle of the night?"

Sean pressed his lips together for a second. "She wouldn't understand," he said, his voice low. "You do."

"I can't come, Sean," I said. "Imagine if my mum found out. I'd be grounded for the rest of my natural life."

"*Please,* Ruby," Sean begged. "I know I shouldn't ask you, but I... I don't have the nerve to go on my own. I need you to come with me. *Please.*"

The microwave pinged and we all jumped, including the dog in my arms.

"There's a phone number on that page," I said hopefully. "Couldn't you just call him?" Sean said nothing as he watched me and waited. I sighed. Maybe the quicker we got this out of the way, the quicker things would go back to normal.

"What's your plan then?" I asked him. "That address is on the other side of LA."

"Remember when you and I were all dressed up at the film premiere and we got a cab across London to Nydia's party?"

"Yes, it's quite hard to forget, what with the swat team they sent after the jewellery I was wearing," I said.

"It's pretty much the same plan. We dress up, we sneak out, we catch a cab."

"You call *that* a plan?" I asked.

"Sorry, Rubes," Sean said, stuffing a handful of buttered popcorn into his mouth and tossing David a kernel. "Haven't you worked out by now that I've only ever got one plan?"

TALENT AGENCIES

The Pat Rivers Talent Agency

25 years of industry experience working with Hollywood's **biggest** stars, the agency that can get your career started and keep you working!

The agent that never sleeps – Open 11am to 11pm!

"Pat Rivers is the hardest working agent in Hollywood!"

Lisa Mitchel, star of *All for One*

Send us your resume and headshot NOW!

The Pat Rivers Talent Agency
1439 N. Gower
Hollywood
CA 90029

e:mail: thepatriverstalentagency@patriverstalent.com
Call: 323 8000 1634 or 1800 MAKE ME FAMOUS
www.patriverstalentagency.com

Chapter Five

Sean and I went back to the screening room. We watched the film for about another twenty minutes before Sean stood up, yawned and stretched.

"I'm going to bed," he said. "Maybe tomorrow I'll feel OK enough to audition."

"That's a good idea," Anne-Marie smiled at him. And then he winked at me when he walked out. Which wasn't all that out of the ordinary. Sean winked at me probably four or five times a day, but just then, just when we were about to sneak out and go and track down his dad in total secrecy, he might as well have had a neon sign on his head flashing "ME AND RUBY HAVE A SECRET!"

I waited for another ten minutes and then tried out my yawn.

"I'm off to bed. Gosh, I am tired!"

Immediately Anne-Marie spun around in her red velvet chair and looked at me.

"That was such a fake yawn, Ruby Parker. What are you trying to cover up?"

"Cover up? Me?" I stared at her for a second. It's well known that lying is not one of my best things. "I am just going to bed, really," I protested weakly. I knew I had "guilty" written all over my face. Thank goodness the screening room was so dark.

"Yeah, yeah. So are you going to cave in and phone Danny, or Hunter, or both?" Anne-Marie teased me. "Do you have a direct line to Sherwood Forest? Hey, maybe there is still a slot for the young Maid Marian..."

"I am not going to phone Danny or Hunter or anyone!" I told her.

"I knew it," Anne-Marie said to Nydia. "I *knew* she still fancied Danny..."

Anne-Marie stopped in her tracks as she noticed that Gabe and Nydia were holding hands.

"Yes," Nydia said, looking sideways at her. "Gabe and I are holding hands. Get over it. And leave Ruby alone. If she wants to phone Danny, it's up to her. You should know it will be about two in the morning at home though, Rubes."

"Well, it doesn't matter, because I'm *not* phoning him," I said as I made my way out of the room.

"Great, so now I'm a gooseberry," I heard Anne-Marie

say through a mouthful of popcorn. I was pretty shocked that both of my friends thought I was still pining after Danny. But at least I could leave the room without any more questions.

Sean and I had agreed that we should dress up a bit to seem like we were going somewhere, which after all we were. I wasn't sure what Sean's definition of dressing up was, but I decided that mine was to wear a dress instead of trousers. I picked a light lilac knee-length dress that I had packed just in case we got invited to any parties and a pair of silver sandals with a low heel that Mum let me wear for special occasions. It was warm outside so I didn't take a jacket. I just brushed my hair, put a little bit of lipgloss on and waited for Sean's secret knock that we'd agreed. One slow, two quick, one slow.

As it was he forgot to knock and just walked in.

"Sean!" I hissed.

Sean stood there and stared at me.

"What?" I said, looking down at myself. "Has it got a stain?"

"No, it's just..." Sean put his hand in his pockets and shrugged. "You look really nice."

"Oh, well, I'm sorry that it's such a shock to you,"

I said, feeling irritated and oddly pleased, and then irritated again. I closed the door behind him.

"That's not what I meant. I meant..."

"It doesn't matter what you meant, Sean," I said, sounding more cross than I intended. "It's gone nine already and we have to get to this address, talk to your dad, if he's there, and get back before anyone notices. Are you sure you don't just want to phone him?"

"No, I have to go there. And anyway – you always look nice, it's just tonight you look even prettier than normal."

I felt my cheeks burn, my tummy screw itself into a tight little knot and my heart start to race.

"Just don't do that, OK," I said to Sean as I went to the door, opening it a crack to check that the coast was clear.

"Do what?" Sean asked.

"Don't notice me or say I'm pretty."

"We're friends, aren't we?" Sean asked. "I was paying a compliment to a friend. I must have told you that you look nice a hundred times."

"No, you haven't actually," I said.

"Well, I should have," Sean said.

"No, you shouldn't," I said, peering down the hall, first one way and then the other.

"But why?"

"Because." I turned round quickly to find that Sean was

standing right behind me and that if he hadn't been a few centimetres taller than me we would have been standing nose to nose. As it was we were standing my nose to his chin. Reluctantly I looked up at him and he smiled down at me.

"Let's just go," I said, backing out into the hall, because despite the high likelihood that I would bump into an adult or a friend, it seemed like the safest option just then.

The adults were all outside sitting around the pool, and Nydia, Gabe and Anne-Marie were still watching the film, so it was easy enough for us to sneak out.

Sean had called a cab company and asked them to pick us up on the corner of the street. As we walked down the road the whole of Hollywood was laid out beneath us, as if the world had turned upside down and the sky full of stars had been laid at our feet.

"One of those twinkling lights belongs to your father," I said to Sean.

"I know," Sean said quietly.

"Sean, he was really, *really* horrible to you," I said. "Are you sure you want to see him?"

"I think so," Sean said, and just as the cab pulled up to the curb he picked up my hand and held it, not letting go for the whole of the journey.

* * *

"Can you wait for us?" Sean asked the driver. He'd been careful not to be Sean Rivers superstar in the car. He switched that part of himself off, like I'd seen him do so many times before. People would walk past him and look at him, and they might think they knew him from somewhere, but they wouldn't know where. But Sean wanted the taxi to wait, and taxis don't wait around for just any old teenager, so I watched in awe as he switched Sean Rivers back on when we got out.

"Sure, I'll wait for you, Sean," the driver said. "My daughter loves you. Will you give me your autograph?"

"No problem," Sean said.

He'd let go of my hand briefly as he gave the driver some money and his signature, but as we turned to face the offices of the Pat Rivers Talent Agency he grabbed it again. It felt strange, my hand in his. Sean and I had been friends for ages now. He often put his arm around me or gave me a hug. It never once seemed strange, or made me feel funny. Of *course* he was holding my hand. He was nervous about seeing his dad and he wanted the support of a good friend, of me. Sean didn't know that for some reason holding hands with him was making my stupid heart race at a million miles an hour. And as long as he *never* knew that I supposed it didn't matter. I'd just have to hope I didn't die of a heart attack before we'd finished visiting his dad.

Sure enough the lights were still on in the agency and there was even a very tired, bored-looking receptionist sitting behind a glass desk in the foyer.

"Sean." I pulled him back just as he was about to walk into the office.

"Yes?" He looked at me.

"Well, your dad's been right here all along, this address has been in the *Yellow Pages* all along. You could have looked him up on the Internet, or phoned him any time. But you didn't. So why now?"

Sean looked up at his father's name displayed in pulsating lights over the doorway. "I miss him, Ruby," he said almost apologetically.

"He bullied you!" I said.

"I know, and I hated him for that, but he's my dad. We were together a long time. I hate him, but I love him and I miss him. I want a dad around. You get that, don't you?"

I nodded. I did get that. When my mum and dad split up, the worst thing about it was Dad not being at home any more. His shoes weren't at the bottom of the stairs; his toothbrush wasn't in the bathroom. It took a really long time to get used to the fact that he was still my dad, only he didn't live in the same place. He told terrible jokes and wore clothes that were far too young for him, but he'd never hit me, or forced me to do something I didn't want to. At the end of the day, I supposed, a dad is a dad, and you love the one you've got even if he's not very nice.

"Come on then," I said, squeezing Sean's fingers. "Let's go in."

"Hi," Sean said to the receptionist, who barely glanced at him over the top of her magazine as we walked up. "Can I see Pat Rivers, please?"

"By appointment only," she said gruffly. "And we don't represent kids any more."

"OK," Sean said, "but I'm not here for an agent. I'm his son – he's my dad. I'm Sean Rivers."

The receptionist dropped her magazine. "Oh my..." She looked from Sean to me, and then back at Sean again. Holding eye contact with Sean as if she were afraid that he might vanish if she blinked, she picked up the phone and pressed a button.

"I know you didn't want to be interrupted, Pat, but your son *Sean* is in reception."

She put the phone down and smiled at us, her lips stretched wide across at least twice the amount of teeth that an average person has.

"He says go right up," she said. "Second floor, turn right."

* * *

"Son!" Sean let go of my hand the instant he saw his dad, probably mostly because Mr Rivers enveloped him in a huge hug. He held Sean pinned to him for quite a long time. When he let go, Sean was red in the face.

"I knew you'd come back to me. I knew that soon you'd realise all that business, it was nothing really. So I got a little obsessed, I know that now. I worked you too hard. I tried to get you to your full potential before you were ready. But I knew that once you'd had some time to think you'd see that you need me."

Sean blinked. "Hi, Dad," he said.

"Well, let's not stay here," Pat Rivers exclaimed. "There's a place down the street that does the best ice-cream milkshakes in California. Let's go celebrate!"

He looked at me as if he'd only just realised I was there.

"Ruby Parker," he said, his smile fading just a little bit. "Can I buy you a milkshake too?"

"Yes please," I said, even though I just wanted to jump back in the cab and go home.

"Well, come on then, kids," Pat Rivers said.

We got in the cab that was waiting for us and drove around the corner to the diner. Sean's dad didn't stop talking the whole way. Sean still hadn't got a word in edgeways by the time we arrived.

"So how is this going to work?" Pat said as we all sat

down. "How do you want to relaunch yourself? To be honest, son, there are so many things that you could do – the world is your oyster. I must get ten calls a week asking me if you would consider a project. All you have to do is say what you want and you will get it, no questions asked."

"Actually, Dad," Sean took a sip of his chocolate milkshake, "I didn't really come over because of work. I made out that I was coming over to screen-test for *Spotlight!...*"

"I heard that!" Mr Rivers exclaimed. "But I knew it couldn't be true because if you were ready to start working again you'd have come to me first. Still, you're here now and that's what counts."

"The thing is," Sean went on, slowly stirring his straw through the thick shake, "I'm *not* ready to start working again. This year has been great. Getting to know Mom again, acting for fun and going to the Academy has been a blast. I get to hang out with friends, and I go to the movies without having to walk down a red carpet. People go past me in the street and they couldn't care less about who I am. I'm not ready to give that up, not yet."

"You know," Mr Rivers said. "This *Spotlight!* movie is going to be huge. That would be the perfect way for you to come back."

My jaw dropped. He was sitting across the table from Sean, staring at him and apparently listening to everything his son said, and yet he couldn't have heard a single word.

"Dad," Sean paused, trying to find the words he wanted to say. "The reason that I came to Hollywood was to see you, not to get work, but because… because I miss you. I don't want a part in a movie or anything else. I just wanted to see you."

I held my breath as Sean and his dad looked at each other across the table. Sean's smile was so sweet and so hopeful that I wanted to fling my arms around him and kiss him. Definitely best not to go there, I decided.

"Does your mother know you're here?" Pat asked after a moment. It was the last thing I expected him to say and by the look on Sean's face he was thinking the same.

"No," he replied. "I didn't want her to try and stop me. It's just me and Ruby."

"I'm glad you came, son," Mr Rivers said, softening his voice. "I've missed you too, of course I have. And, well, if you don't want to work any more then I'm fine with that. Like I said, I know I worked you too hard in the past. I know I drove you away. I don't want to lose you again."

His face sort of crumpled as if he were trying not to

cry and I realised then exactly who it was that Sean inherited his acting skills from.

"Really?" Sean asked, his face lighting up. "You miss me too?"

"Of course," Mr Rivers said, sniffing. "You're my only son." He reached a hand across the table and clapped it on Sean's shoulder. "It's probably best you don't tell your mother for a while though."

"Why?" I asked, speaking before I remembered that I was only supposed to be there for moral support and was not to get involved.

"Because, Miss Parker," Mr River said, narrowing his eyes slightly, "Sean and I need some time to get to know each other again." He looked at Sean. "He needs to know he can trust me. Sean, we will tell your mom, it would be wrong not to, but after we've had some bonding time – right, son?"

I resisted the urge to shove my fingers down my throat and took a large slurp of milkshake instead.

"Right," Sean said happily.

"So have you taken the screen test for *Spotlight!* yet?" Mr Rivers asked after a couple of seconds.

"No," Sean told him. "I mean, I was never going to take it. I only said I would to get Mom to bring me over here."

"But you still could if you wanted too, right?"

"Yeah, I *could*..." Sean said hesitantly.

"I'm just thinking, it takes a long time to cast a musical. There'll be all sorts of stuff they have to do before filming starts. Find the kids with the right chemistry. Workshop it with the actors, rehearsing, staging the dance scenes, choreography, singing, coaching..."

"So?" Sean asked him, perplexed.

"Well, if you don't even test for a role you'll be back in England within a week. But if you test for the film and get a part you'll be here for weeks. We could spend some serious time together."

"But I don't want to be in *Spotlight!*" Sean said.

"I know that, son, but if you make out that you do, go along with it, we would be able to see more of each other. And you'd be giving me the chance to make things up to you, to really be a good dad. You can pull out of the film later on, say you've changed your mind at any time. You're Sean Rivers after all. You can do what you like."

"Except it's not very fair to pretend to take a part when you..." I started to interfere again, but Sean spoke over me.

"OK," he said. My jaw dropped open for a second time and I stared at him.

"Sean!"

"OK, I'll take the audition, and if I get offered a part..."

"Oh, you will," Pat Rivers said, and he was probably right.

"Then I'll stick around for as long as I can, but only until they start rehearsing properly. I'm not going to sign any kind of contract, because I'm serious. I don't want to be famous any more, Dad."

"Son, there are some things you can't change," Mr Rivers told him with a glint of triumph in his eye.

"We'd better get back before we're missed," I said, looking at my watch. Besides I wanted a word alone with Sean.

"Here's my personal number..." Pat Rivers pushed a business card across the table to Sean. "I'll see you soon, OK?"

"OK!" Sean said, grinning happily.

"Come on," I said. "The cab's still waiting. I hope we've got enough money..."

As we stepped out into the night air Sean hugged me so tightly that my feet left the ground.

"Sean!" I said, feeling flustered. "Stop doing that!"

"But I always hug you," Sean said happily.

"I know, but not now, not when both of us are supposed to be at home in bed and no one – including your girlfriend and my mum – knows that we're here. It makes me feel... odd."

"I'm sorry, Rubes," Sean said, with a shrug that proved he wasn't. "It's just that it's worked out exactly the way I hoped. Dad was really happy to see me and he doesn't care that I don't want to work any more. I think when I left him to go live with Mom, it really made him see what matters."

"Are you sure about that?" I asked him as we climbed back into the cab.

"Yes, of course. He said so – didn't he?" Sean said.

"Yes, he did. It's just that, well – Sean, he's got you to do something that no one, not your mum, not Sylvia Lighthouse, not even Anne-Marie, has been able to do. He's got you to audition for a film."

It's Your Life!

The Inside Scoop on the inside information. Who's on the way up and who's on the way out!

★ ★ ★ ★ ★ ★ ★ ★ ★ ★ ★ ★

Kirsty O'Brien—our fave girl TV Star can do no wrong! The critics love her and so do we. Here's hoping Kirsty kills on the set of the new movie production of *Spotlight!*

Sean Rivers—Sean's back and we have three readers' cell phone snaps to prove it. Sean's in Hollywood again and rumors are rife that he'll be returning to the big screen again. Please make those rumors come true, Sean. IYL! misses you and so do all the girls of America!

Danny Harvey—You've never heard of him and neither have we, but in the UK he's a top TV and recording star. Watch this space—Inside Scoop predicts big things for Danny Harvey.

Ruby Parker—Remember Ruby? Our fave young Brit is back to try out for a role in *Spotlight!* Since you voted *The Lost Treasure of King Arthur* as your DVD of the Year, we're sure that young Ruby is shooting towards stardom.

↑ **UP!** ↑

Down!

Adrienne Charles—We're so over Adrienne here at IYL! Turns out the rumors about her bullying other kids at her school were true—that's NOT cool, Adrienne!

Hunter Blake—Never thought we'd ever see *Hollywood High's* Hunter over this side of Inside Scoop, but rumor has it that he's being acted off the set of his new movie by British newbie **Danny Harvey!** Here's hoping you get your groove back, Hunter...

Henry Dufault—What is it about Henry that means he can't stay out of trouble? This talented actor has been asked to leave his latest school again after an incident with a fire hydrant. We say, Henry, why can't you just calm down? You don't have to be a rebel for us to notice you.

Chapter Six

"I'm not mentioned in this magazine either!" Anne-Marie said, as she pored over the copy of *It's Your Life!* that Mum had brought home to take our minds off things while we waited to find out if any of us were going to be called back for the next round of auditions. "I know it's an American mag, but you'd have thought they would have spotted my talent by now. I was the star of the TV version of *Spotlight!*, or one of them anyway, *and* I'm Sean Rivers' girlfriend! When are people going to start noticing *me*?"

We were sitting by the pool trying hard not to listen for the phone. Waiting for news of an audition is one of the worst and best things that I have ever done. It's a weird mixture of excitement, hope, terror and disappointment because you try to be ready for whatever the result is.

And this morning it was even harder to wait for two reasons. Firstly because it wasn't only me that was waiting for news – it was my two best friends as well – and secondly because I had hardly had time to think about what had happened last night with Sean and his dad.

Somehow the two of us had made it home and back to our rooms without being caught, but that didn't make me feel any better about what had happened. Mr Rivers had seemed as if he meant what he said about wanting Sean back in his life, and Sean was so happy. But I couldn't help feeling that Mr Rivers was going to end up using and hurting Sean again. I just didn't know how to explain that to Sean, and so far this morning I hadn't had a chance to talk to him as he hadn't come down yet.

"Why haven't they mentioned me?" Anne-Marie was still complaining. "They've mentioned Sean and Hunter Blake – even Danny! And you, Ruby, they never seem to shut up about you, but not me. Why don't they *ever* mention me?"

"They haven't mentioned me this time either," Nydia offered.

"What does a girl have to do to get famous around here?" Anne-Marie slapped the magazine down on the table.

"Don't ask me," I said with a shrug. "I did practically everything wrong the last time I was in Hollywood."

"I need to get Sean to go out somewhere in public

with me." There was no stopping Anne-Marie in this frame of mind. "Maybe I can get him to take me shopping on Rodeo Drive, and we'd be bound to get snapped by the paps, wouldn't we, Rubes? Like that time they took that photo of your mum and wrote all those horrible things about her. If I can get Sean to be seen out with me, they'd have to find out who I am and then they'd write about me."

"You might not want them to write about you, Anne-Marie," my mum said as she came to join us. She was carrying the cordless phone in her hand, as if she normally took it all round the house with her and wasn't waiting for a special call that would determine all of our futures at all.

"Well, they wouldn't write anything rude about *me*!" Anne-Marie reasoned. "I look great!"

"Morning," Gabe said, wandering out to join us and blinking in the sunshine. "What's happening today then? Why's everyone so hyper?"

"Oh, Gabe," Nydia said, grinning at him. "We're waiting for the studio to call. Today we either find out we've got through to the next stage or we get packed off back home."

"Home I hope," Gabe said, grabbing a glass of orange juice and yawning. "It's too sunny over here. If I get back before the end of next week I'll be in time for the preseason trials at football camp."

"You seem like you're in a hurry to go home," Anne-Marie said, raising a brow.

Gabe smiled at Nydia. "There are some good things about Hollywood," he said, making Anne-Marie and me clutch our throats and gag.

"Girls, that's enough!" Mum said, chuckling. Just then the phone began trilling in her hand and she almost dropped it. "Goodness!" she said, putting a hand to her chest and looking at it.

"Is that the studio?" Sean's mum came in and stared at the phone too.

"That will be news," Mr Martinez said, emerging from the TV room.

All of us stared at the ringing telephone.

"Shouldn't someone actually answer it?" Anne-Marie asked finally.

Mum jumped into life. "Hello? Yes, this is Mrs Parker. Yes, you can tell me the news for all of the children...."

Twenty minutes later, after Mum had shared the news, we all sat around the pool and looked at each other. We didn't know how to act.

"It's completely fine, honest," Gabe said. "I knew they weren't going to call me back. I got in there with Anne-Marie and I sort of froze. But you lot should be psyched! You're all going back and it's well cool, man." He grinned and winked at Nydia. "I'm pleased for you."

"The boy's right," Mr Martinez said. "I don't think Gabe's mum and sisters would have been that pleased if we'd stayed out here the whole summer. But you girls getting through is brilliant news!"

"It is, isn't it?" Nydia said, looking at me, the start of a smile curling the corners of her mouth. "This means that the three of us have already beaten at least two hundred people! Now there's got to be only about fifty going for the lead roles. We're that close to getting a lead part in a Hollywood film!"

"Well, I'm not surprised," Anne-Marie said. "I knew we'd be brilliant – especially me!"

"So what do we have to do next?" I asked. I felt sort of odd, as if the news wasn't really real. It was incredibly exciting news and it took us one step nearer to a part in the film. A film that could change all of our careers forever and make us truly global stars. But I decided it was best not to think about any of that. After all, in show business things have a habit of going wrong when you least expect them. I knew that better than anyone.

"They've asked that you go in tomorrow for audition workshops," Mum told us. "They'll try you out in different groups. Test you to see which actors work best together. I think there are all sorts – singing, dance, acting. It will be a long day, but a fabulous one. I'll phone the Academy and tell Ms Lighthouse. She'll be thrilled!"

"Morning," Sean greeted us as he ambled out to the pool. "I heard the phone," he said as he stretched. "Good news?"

"For everyone but me," Gabe said with a shrug. "And that's kind of good news anyway."

"Well, I have some news too," Sean said.

I sat up a bit and looked at him. Was he going to tell his mum about seeing his dad? On the one hand I sort of hoped he was, but on the other I was imagining the seventy-five years or so that I would be grounded for sneaking out of the house and going across Hollywood late at night.

"I feel fine today," Sean said. "So if the studio can fit me in for a screen test then I'm ready."

"Are you sure? Why would you want to do that?" I asked him, perhaps a little too quickly.

"Why? Because it's what he's here for, Ruby!" Anne-Marie told me, jumping up and hugging Sean. "This is brilliant news, Sean! Do you want me to come with you?"

Sean smiled at her. "No, you stay here and rest. You'll need all your energy for tomorrow. I'll go in with Mom. It'll be cool."

Mrs Rivers looked at Sean for a long moment and then put her arm around his shoulder.

"Are you sure that this is what you want, Sean?" she asked him, looking into his eyes. "Only when you came down with that sore throat yesterday I thought it was nature's way of telling us you weren't ready to act again. The only person you have to do this for is you. What I or Anne-Marie or the whole world thinks isn't important. Is it, Anne-Marie?"

"Um, well... no, no, it's not," Anne-Marie frowned, but agreed.

"Only do this if it's what you really, really want," Sean's mum told him.

Sean paused and I wondered if I was the only one who could see the mixture of guilt and worry on his face. But then he turned on his world-famous Sean Rivers smile and it made us believe the impossible.

"Mom," he said, "this is what I really, *really* want."

"We've got a whole day with nothing to do," Anne-Marie said, after we had all waved Sean off, wishing him luck and telling him we hoped he'd break a leg. "Shall we go shopping?"

"Not me," Nydia said as we walked back into the house. "I haven't got any money and besides...." She looked over to where Gabe was playing football with his dad. "Gabe's flying back tomorrow."

"When *did* you decide that you liked Gabe, by the way?" I asked Nydia. We had trailed into the TV room and Anne-Marie had put C! the Celebrity Channel on. "And what happened to Greg? You never said you were going to chuck him."

"I didn't chuck him really," Nydia said. "We just stopped calling and texting. Then when me and Gabe were suddenly thrown into the leads for *Spotlight!*, we got on really well..."

"Has he been your secret boyfriend all this time?" Anne-Marie challenged her.

"No!" Nydia said. "I didn't say anything because I didn't know if he liked me, and anyway, after the show I didn't really see him. But when we came out here and we hung out a bit, he asked me out, if you must know!"

"Of course we must know, we're your best friends! It's the law that you tell us everything," I said, instantly feeling guilty about what I had not told Anne-Marie. "Anyway I think it's cool."

"It is sweet," Anne-Marie agreed. "Sean was my secret boyfriend when we started going out together. Do you remember – when the whole world thought it was Ruby he liked?" Anne-Marie giggled as if the idea of Sean liking me was impossible. Which it was, I supposed. "Me and Sean are a perfect couple."

"Really?" I asked her, worried about how interested I sounded, not to mention felt. "How do you know?"

"Because..." Anne-Marie trailed off as she thought about it. "Just look at us!" she exclaimed.

"Do you, you know... like, love him?" I asked her.

She laughed, tossing her golden curls over her shoulder. "Yes, I do. I love that he's going to go and audition for a part in *Spotlight! The Movie Musical.* I love that he makes me laugh and that when we walk down the road together every other girl within a five-mile radius practically drops dead from jealousy. He's perfect for me and I'm perfect for him."

"But *are* you?" I asked thoughtfully.

"Pardon?" said Anne-Marie.

"I mean you are," I said hastily. "You are perfect for him, of course. Come on then – let's go shopping."

Anne-Marie can shop better than anyone else I know. Maybe it helps that she has a lot of money, or that her mother is a fashion designer and her dad is a movie producer. But I don't think it's any of that. I think it's just in her genes – like Gabe can keep a football up in the air longer than anyone else in the school and Nydia can sing a top C without even having to try that hard. Anne-Marie is good at a lot of things, but shopping is her natural gift.

As we went from Guess to Banana Republic, Gap and Esprit, and all the other cool shops that seemed so much better here than they did at home, Anne-Marie scanned the rails like a hawk looking for prey. She didn't browse or um and ah over things. She just knew what to pick up and she was never wrong. And it wasn't just for herself – she picked out outfits for me and Nydia too. She knew all our measurements, down to our shoes, and she knew exactly what colours suited all of us.

"You're best in berry colours," she said, holding a deep purple dress up against me. "I suit pastels and white. And Nydia, well, she can wear almost any colour. Let's get you this dress and her this yellow one – she will look so cute in it!"

"We can't afford these," I said, checking the tag.

"I can," Anne-Marie said, waving her mum's charge card at me. "Mummy sent me this so I could take care of my expenses while I was here."

"I don't think your expenses include buying clothes for your friends," I said.

"No, but she won't know that. She probably won't even read the statement," Anne-Marie said, suddenly looking quite sad. "I'm going to buy them anyway, so you'll have to wear them otherwise it will be a waste."

She sounded like a spoilt brat, but I could see from looking at her that the thought of an endless pot of money didn't make her happy.

"Have you heard from your mum?" I asked.

Anne-Marie had been certain that she would see her mum while she was in Hollywood. She'd been secretly looking forward to it ever since we all found out we were coming. She hadn't said anything; she wasn't the sort of person to talk about personal feelings all that much. But ever since we'd arrived she'd been checking her phone for messages and missed calls, or asking if anyone had called for her. So far nobody had.

"No," Anne-Marie sighed, sitting down suddenly on the edge of a pedestal usually reserved for mannequins. I settled down next to her and put my arm around her. "Nothing, not an e-mail or anything. I left her a message about us getting called back for second auditions, but she hasn't replied."

"What about your dad?"

Anne-Marie shook her head. "He's in Budapest. I knew I wasn't going to see him, but Mummy said she'd come if she could. Oh, look, I'm being ridiculous. I'm sure she'll visit – I just wish she'd call and tell me when..."

"You miss her, don't you?" I asked. It was hard for me to imagine Anne-Marie with her mum, because I'd never actually met her properly. She wasn't like my mum, Nydia's or even Sean's. Mums that were almost a part of my daily life. She was a bit like those photos that are already in a photo frame when you buy it from a shop. You know the person in the picture isn't real. And that's how I felt about Anne-Marie's mum; she didn't seem real.

A few years ago I remember her coming to an open day at the Academy. She was tall like Anne-Marie, with the same curly blonde hair. She had arrived, breezed around the school as if she owned it and then left. And I think she might have left without saying goodbye to Anne-Marie although I wasn't sure.

My mum was always around whether I wanted her to be or not.

"I don't know if I miss her," Anne-Marie said quietly. "I miss having a mum like yours. Someone to tell me what to do, to talk about stuff with. But the weird thing is, Ruby, I don't know if I miss *my* mum or just *a* mum.

After all I hardly ever see her. I don't blame her or anything. Some mums are more mumsy than others... but I just sometimes wish...." She looked at me sideways. "Can I tell you something?" she asked.

"Of course," I said.

"You know when you asked me if I love Sean?" I nodded. "Well, I made a joke of it because I didn't want to look silly. But the truth is I do love him, and you, and Nydia. I love all three of you because you are like my family. You're the only people in the world who really care what happens to me. I know I tease you and act like a diva and spend most of my time being a horrible, self-obsessed cow. But I don't know what I'd do without the three of you. And if you ever tell anyone I said that I'll kill you."

"Well, you won't have to find out what you'd do without us because we'll always be friends," I said hugging her back, a huge well of guilt brimming up inside me. OK, so I'd recently started feeling a bit odd around Sean. Thankfully no one ever had to know that, including Sean. But how would Anne-Marie feel if, *when,* she found out that I had been keeping Sean's secret; that he had trusted me and not her? She'd feel like two of the three people in the world that she relied on had let her down, and she didn't deserve that. I had to make Sean talk to her tonight. I had to make everything right as soon as I possibly could.

"Anything I can do to cheer you up?" I asked.

"How about double-chocolate-chip-cookie ice cream?" she ventured. "I saw this ice-cream parlour across the street that looks amazing."

"It's a deal," I said. As I hauled her up on to her feet I stumbled backwards and straight into the person who was behind me. Knocking him off his feet, the pair of us staggered backwards, tumbling on to the floor and taking a clothes rack with us.

"That works too!" Anne-Marie laughed.

"Help me, I'm stuck under teen casual wear!" I yelled. But Anne-Marie was laughing too much to be of any use. It took two shop assistants and another customer to get us free from the rack.

I sat up, disentangling myself from dresses and the arms and legs of the poor person I had landed on, apologising all the time.

"I'm so sorry, I don't know what happened. I just lost my balance and then splat! And there you were right behind me and you sort of got caught in the crossfire... I really hope you haven't broken anything because I did land right on top of you and..."

"Seriously, Ruby, it's fine," came a familiar voice.

I stopped talking and finally got a look at the person I had landed on.

"You!" I shouted, making the whole shop look at me. I must have concussion, I thought. Or maybe post-traumatic stress disorder, because the person I had landed on appeared to be Danny Harvey.

Chapter Seven

"Anne-Marie, call 911, I'm hallucinating," I said.

"No, you're not, Rubes," Anne-Marie said. "That actually is Danny."

"I was just on my way to meet a friend when I spotted you though the window," Danny said. "So I thought I'd come in and say hello."

"But you're supposed to be in Sherwood Forest!" I said.

"We were never going to film in the real Sherwood Forest," Danny said a few minutes later when the three of us sat down for ice cream and I was just about getting my head round seeing him in the very last place I expected. "There's not enough of it left to film in, and the little bit there is, is protected by the National Trust. Most of it's being shot in Romania, but we're in Hollywood for a few weeks to do some special effects and studio scenes."

"Honestly, Ruby, for one so experienced in the film industry you are naïve," Anne-Marie teased me. "You should have seen your face when you realised it was Danny you squashed – it was spectacular!"

"You were the one who said I didn't have to worry about Danny and Hunter because they were miles away in Sherwood Forest..." I trailed off as I realised what I had just said. "Not that I was remotely worried about you and Hunter or anything anyway," I added.

"So how is it working with the lovely Hunter?" Anne-Marie asked Danny as she scooped up a big spoonful of ice cream. "Does he talk about Ruby?"

Danny blushed, studying his mobile phone as he got a text. "No, not really," he said. He looked at me for a long moment and then seemed to decide something. "The first day I met him it was all a bit awkward and then he said we had to clear the air about you. He said that he really liked you, but that you didn't feel the same way, and I said that now you and me are just friends. So once we got that clear everything was cool and now we're mates. He said to say hi."

"Oh, right, well, tell him hi back," I said, waving my hand at no one. It was all a bit of a shock to be honest, literally bumping into Danny the way that I did and then hearing him bluntly telling me what I had been wondering on and off for months. It was officially over between us. We were just friends. As it happened I was quite relieved. But that didn't stop the whole experience being really, really odd.

As Danny and Anne-Marie chatted about Sean and his decision to take the screen test for *Spotlight!* I tried to look at Danny without him noticing so that I could test out how he made me feel. It was strange. I had expected to feel flustered and anxious, and for my cheeks to go pink and my heart to race. But actually the more I looked at him, the more I realised it was just nice to see him. Just like seeing an old friend.

"So tell us – who else are you acting with? Who's playing the part of young Marian?"

"Oh, um, that's Kirsty," Danny said, smiling. "Kirsty O'Brien. She's really cool."

"What's she been in?" Anne-Marie asked him.

"*At Home with Dad* – a kids' sitcom," Danny told her. "She's really cool."

"You said that once already," Anne-Marie said with a tiny smile.

"I know," Danny said. "She just texted me to tell me she's got through the first round of auditions for *Spotlight!* too."

"She's doing two films at once?" I asked him. "How is that possible?"

"She's shot most of her scenes for *Robin Hood* already

and has six months before we finish the location stuff – she's very in demand. *It's Your Life!* calls her Hollywood's Fastest Rising Star."

"Oh, right," I said, glancing at Anne-Marie. "Maybe we'll meet her tomorrow."

"Actually you're going to meet her in about five seconds," Danny said, smiling at someone who was walking up behind me. "She's the friend I was going to meet."

"Hi, Dan!" A blonde girl with brown eyes and a sparkly smile greeted Danny and slid into the seat next to him. As soon as I saw her I recognised her face from the sitcom that Nydia and I had not been watching yesterday.

"Kirsty, this is Ruby and Anne-Marie – friends from home. They're auditioning for *Spotlight!* too."

"Hi, it's so great to meet you," Kirsty said, smiling at us. "I know exactly who you are. *You* are Ruby Parker. I love *The Lost Treasure of King Arthur* – I've seen it about a hundred times. And *you* are Anne-Marie Chance. I've watched your performance in the British version of *Spotlight!* – you were brilliant, a real inspiration."

"And you are unexpectedly likeable," Anne-Marie said. "So are you two an item now?"

"Um," Danny stared quite hard into his ice cream and

blushed. Kirsty clapped her hand over her face and giggled.

"What? Did I say something wrong?" Anne-Marie asked innocently.

"We're really just friends," Kirsty said, smiling sideways at Danny in the universal girl-signal that meant she'd like to be more. "So far."

"Well, anyway," I said, sensing that Danny might implode from embarrassment. "We need to be getting back home. I expect we'll see you tomorrow, Kirsty."

"Looking forward to it," Kirsty beamed.

"I bet you are," Anne-Marie said.

Sapphire Blue Productions

FAX

TO: Mrs Janice Parker

FROM: Christina Darcy, Casting Director

RE: Audition workshops for RUBY PARKER, ANNE-MARIE CHANCE, NYDIA ASSIMIN

Dear Mrs Parker,

Please find attached the parental permission forms required by Sapphire Blue Productions before the next stage of casting can commence. Please ensure that each form is signed by a parent or legal guardian.

The workshop process will begin tomorrow at 9 a.m. at Sapphire Blue Productions Rehearsal Studio on Delrado Blvd. Address and map are attached. Please make sure that the children are wearing comfortable clothing, bring their dance shoes with them and one piece of prepared music as they will be asked to sing a solo.

We look forward to seeing you all tomorrow,
Yours sincerely

Christina Darcy

Chapter Eight

When we got back from shopping, Mum and Nydia were in the kitchen reading the fax. Anne-Marie and I grabbed it out of their hands and read it out loud.

"Parental consent forms?" Anne-Marie made a face. "Will you be able to sign those for me, Mrs Parker? I don't need an actual parent to sign them, do I?"

"Well, your mum has agreed for me to look after you while we are here, so I don't see why not," Mum said. "But if it has to be an actual parent, I'm sure we'll be able to fax the forms to your mum or dad to be signed."

"If you can find them," Anne-Marie said, looking at me.

"Shouldn't we be focusing on this part?" I said, picking up the fax. "The bit where it says we have to have a piece of music prepared because they are going to ask us to sing a solo!"

"Yes, I was wondering about that," Mum said dubiously. "You can sing something from *Spotlight!*, can't you?"

"Except that everyone will be doing that," Anne-Marie replied thoughtfully. "We need something different… Hey, maybe we can get Danny to come over and teach us the words to 'You Take Me To (Kensington Heights)'!"

"Danny?" Nydia looked confused.

"Turns out he's not in Sherwood," I told her. "He's in Beverly Hills."

"And he's got a new girlfriend," Anne-Marie added.

"She's not his girlfriend," I said.

"Only because he's too dim to ask her out," Anne-Marie said, rolling her eyes. "But she looks like the kind of girl who gets what she wants, so I shouldn't think it will be long…"

"What? Where? *Who?*" Nydia asked all at once. As we filled her in on how we met Danny and Kirsty O'Brien, Mum peered in Jeremy's giant fridge, probably hoping that we would forget she was there so she could listen to every word.

"That must have been a bit freaky," Nydia said after Anne-Marie told her all about Kirsty. "What's she like?"

I looked at both of my friends and said, "She seemed really nice actually and as for her and Danny…" I glanced towards the fridge where Mum was apparently fascinated by a tub of yoghurt. "I just don't mind any more."

"Which is a good job," Mum said, unable to keep quiet any longer. "Because you have to learn a song each by tomorrow and I haven't played piano since 1994. We'd better get practising!"

I was trying my hardest to learn 'Good Morning Baltimore' from *Hairspray* when Sean and his mum came back. Anne-Marie's shrieks of excitement were louder than my singing so thankfully Mum stopped torturing Jeremy's piano and we went to find out what all the fuss was about. Everyone was in the hallway with Sean when we arrived.

"You got through?" I asked Sean as soon as I saw him.

"Sort of," he said, looking uncomfortable. Anne-Marie had her arm hooked through his and was grinning like a Cheshire cat.

"Sort of? What does that mean?" I asked him.

"It means," Sean's mum said, putting her arm around Sean and hugging him to her, "that they have offered Sean the part of Sebastian in *Spotlight! The Movie Musical* and that Sean has accepted."

"Subject to contract," Sean said, looking at me.

"Oh, Sean, stop sounding like an agent and start getting excited – you've got the lead!" Anne-Marie said.

"This is HUGE. I can't wait to tell Jade and Menakshi – this is going to kill them. I might e-mail them now actually, or maybe text as it's a special occasion..."

"You mean he doesn't have to do any more auditions?" Nydia asked.

"No, he's got the part," Mrs Rivers told us. "They said that if there was anyone in the world they could cast in that role it would be Sean, and that was that."

"But you've been gone all day," I said.

"There were a lot of people to meet," Sean said with a shrug. It was weird – everyone else in the room probably thought he was being shy and modest about his success. But I knew he was feeling bad. Bad about lying to his mum, to Anne-Marie, to the studio and, worst of all, to himself. I knew he didn't want to play Sebastian; he didn't want the lead role in any film with all of the attention and stress it would bring him. I knew he was only doing this because his dad had somehow made him think it was a good idea, and I couldn't understand why he wouldn't see how mad he was being.

But I couldn't say any of that, so instead I just smiled and shrugged, "Well done."

"So when you go back for the workshops tomorrow, Sean will be there working with all the different groups."

"This is fantastic," Anne-Marie said. "Because you know what this means, don't you?"

We all looked at her. "What?" I asked.

"Well, the girl who's picked to play Arial will be the girl that Sean has most onscreen chemistry with – and it's bound to be me, isn't it? I'm going to get the part of Arial!"

"Well, maybe," I said uncertainly.

"You've as good a chance as any," my mum said.

"Of course I will," Anne-Marie said happily. "Sean just has to tell them he wants me to play Arial and they'll give me the part."

"Except that wouldn't be exactly fair..." Nydia said uncertainly.

"Yes, well, show business isn't fair, is it?" Anne-Marie said. "That's sort of the whole point."

"I don't think so, Annie," Sean said. "And anyway I don't have much say in who else they cast. I just get to sit in on the auditions. They told me today I'd be working with at least twenty potential Arials tomorrow."

"Oh." Anne-Marie looked crestfallen for about one millionth of a second and then she started jumping around again. "It doesn't matter anyway, because me and Sean are bound to work the best together. It's going to be brilliant!"

"We should celebrate!" Gabe said. "Me going home, Sean getting a lead role."

"A small, quiet celebration that involves an early night," Mum said, getting supporting nods from Sean's mum and Mr Martinez. "How about pizzas and ice cream all round?"

She put her hands over her ears as we all cheered.

Later on, as Anne-Marie was still speculating on exactly when they would be offering her the part of Arial, I walked out into the garden for a think. It was still really warm and quiet out by the pool. All I could hear were crickets in the shrubbery and the distant sound of music from inside where Nydia was still practising her song while my mum murdered the sheet music. David had come out with me and was trotting at my heels, sniffing around in the plants and occasionally growling at something that was clearly not there. David never growled at anything that really was there: those things he hid from.

I sat on the edge of one of the sunloungers by the pool and looked into the dark water. A lot had happened since we'd arrived in Hollywood and, for once, not a lot of it had happened to me. I'd been feeling so worried and nervous about coming back here after the last time, but I'd hardly had a second to think about me. Tomorrow might include one of the most important auditions I would ever have, and the very first proper one since I decided I didn't want to give up acting after all, but somehow that didn't seem as important as everything else that was going on. Mainly this huge great big secret that Sean was keeping from everyone else; a secret I didn't know how to keep for much longer. Once before I'd given away a secret that belonged to Sean and it could have ruined his life. I wasn't sure if he'd forgive me a second time.

"Whatcha thinking?" Sean asked me, making me jump as he stepped out of the shadow of the veranda.

"I'm thinking about you," I said before I knew it.

"Can't blame you," Sean said with a grin. "I am fascinating."

I pursed my lips just to be sure that I didn't return his infectious smile.

"Sean, I'm serious," I told him. "I'm thinking about you keeping seeing your dad a secret from your mum, and about how you're lying to both your mum and Anne-Marie about why you took the part of Sebastian. Your dad said there'd be weeks of auditions and rehearsals. But you got the part, Sean. You've got the lead role in a major movie and you don't really want it." I made myself look into his eyes. "Sean, what are you doing?"

Sean sat down alongside me on the sunlounger and looked into the pool.

"I don't know," he said, after a moment. "But I like that you worry about me."

"Be serious!" I said, feeling annoyed.

"I am serious," Sean said, glancing at me. "All I wanted to do was to see my dad, to get close to him again. I never meant for this to happen. But now that it has, it'll give me some more time to get to know him again and to get Mom ready for the idea that I want him back in my life."

"And pretending to take the lead role in the world's biggest teen movie musical ever was the best way you could think of doing that?" I asked him.

"It was the way it happened," Sean said.

"Well, it's the wrong way," I said firmly. "Sean, you *have* to tell your mum the truth. *And* Anne-Marie – before this goes any further and you really get in deep. Anne-Marie's your girlfriend and my best friend. It's not right to lie to her or your mum – plus it's really stupid."

"I know," Sean said. He was quiet for a long time and we sat there in silence, until David decided that some imaginary monster was lurking underneath our sunlounger and launched an assault on our toes.

"It's been kind of fun though," Sean said when David

finally abandoned our feet and tried instead to murder a towel. I frowned.

"What do you mean?" I asked.

"Having something that just you and me know about," Sean said.

"That's just silly," I told him.

"Look..." Sean trailed off for a second and then took a breath and went on. "Anne-Marie is so cool, she's a great girl and I really like her, but I sort of think that me and her... Well, I think we're more just friends really than boyfriend and girlfriend."

"I don't think she thinks that!" I whispered crossly, worried that Anne-Marie might somehow hear us through an open window, even though the chances of that seemed slim since the parents had now started singing. Clearly no one in this house had inherited their singing ability from anyone present.

"I'm not so sure," Sean said. "I know she likes the idea of dating a star, but I'm not so sure she really likes me. I was famous when we met and ever since then she's wanted me to be famous again. If I was just any kid would she even notice me?"

"Of course she would, you're gorgeous!" I exclaimed before I realised what I'd said. "Obviously *I* don't think that. I mean, you've come top in the Top Ten Teen Hunk

Totty poll for the last two years, so that's just a fact."

Sean shook his head, "Ruby, the thing is..."

"The thing is what?" I asked him, impatiently tapping my foot.

"You've never treated me like other girls do," Sean told me.

"So?" I said sulkily. "And?"

"You didn't go crazy when you met me and act all silly as if you'd lost your brain. We just got on and had fun, and you don't care if I'm famous or just another kid at a stage school, and I really like that about you."

"Well, that's what friends are for," I said, miserably thinking how I'd done a lot of acting as if I didn't have a brain recently, only Sean hadn't even noticed, which for some reason made me feel more confused..

"I've always felt like you really got me," Sean said. "And then the other day when we snuck out to find Dad, it hit me. This hugely, massively obvious thing that I've somehow been missing all along."

"What hit you?" I asked him wide-eyed.

"It's *you* I like," Sean said.

I shook my head. "I like you too, Sean, but you've still got to..."

"No, I mean I *really* like you, Ruby. I mean I wish *you* were my girlfriend."

"I... *what?*" I asked him, hearing my voice rise in a shriek that could shatter glass.

"You heard me," Sean said, a tiny smile curling up one side of this mouth.

"B-b... but you can't say that." I struggled to get my words out. "You can't say— Just don't say it, OK? Anne-Marie is my best friend and your girlfriend, and anyway you're wrong. She cares about you a lot. She told me today how much you mean to her. I *can't* be your girlfriend, Sean."

"OK," Sean said, looking over his shoulder as if he could see something in the dusk. When he looked back at me I nearly had to sit down again. Instead I took a couple of steps away from him, wondering how I could get back inside with the others, back to my life where I didn't have to think about any of these things.

"Look," Sean said, "I can see that right now it seems impossible..."

"Right now and forever," I reminded him firmly.

"But say I hadn't met Anne-Marie a year ago. Say that back then it had just been me and you, and we'd hung out and got to know each other and realised how much we liked each other right about now, and I asked you to go on a date with me..."

"But that's not how it is," I said more quietly as Sean took two steps nearer. I was sure David could hear my heart thundering in my chest, because he'd stopped barking and was sitting perfectly still with his head cocked to one side, staring at me.

"But if it was," Sean said, "and I asked you to be my girlfriend, what would you say?" Suddenly he seemed very close and I realised exactly what people mean about having their heart in their mouth.

"I..." I don't know what I was going to say because suddenly we were interrupted.

"Guys!" Nydia came tearing out to the pool and stopped dead when she saw Sean and me standing face to face.

"Sorry," I said, leaping away from him as if he had just given me an electric shock. "We're just... rehearsing. Sean asked me to rehearse with him."

"Oh, right, OK," Nydia said slowly. She looked from me to Sean and back again, with a frown on her face. "Anyway you have to come and see Mr Martinez and your mum singing 'I've Had the Time of My Life'. It's the most hilarious and scary thing I have ever seen."

"Coming," I said. But I didn't move.

"What now?" Nydia asked me.

"I've just got to get my... thing," I said, gesturing in the direction of the pool where I saw David killing a towel again. "Got to rescue my towel."

"Your towel." Nydia gave me a long look that let me know she knew there was something else going on. "See you inside then."

She turned on her heel and went back indoors.

"Stop being so... silly," I said to Sean before he could say another word. "I would *never* have gone out with you." Then I pounded along the path after Nydia.

And it *was* funny watching my mum and Mr Martinez singing a duet, while my mum played the piano badly. It was cringingly, hilariously, dreadfully funny, but I couldn't laugh because all I could think about was that my life kept on getting more and more complicated, and there didn't seem to be anything I could do about it.

That wasn't funny at all.

Spotlight! The Movie Musical

Program of Events for Group Audition workshops

9–11 a.m.

You will be called in individually to meet the producers, casting directors and some cast members. You will then have a Polaroid photo taken (subject to applicable parental consent forms).

11–12 p.m.

You will perform your musical piece and read a script provided by the panel.

12–1 p.m.

Break for lunch.

1–3 p.m.

You will be put into groups of six to workshop scenes and numbers from Spotlight! The Movie Musical. You will be assigned a rehearsal director. Groups are non-negotiable unless your rehearsal director tells you to move.

3–5 p.m.

Your group will perform for the selection panel.

Sapphire Blue Productions thanks you for your patience and participation in this process.

Chapter Nine

The first bad thing to happen the next day was that Anne-Marie was not allowed to audition. The second thing was that I lost my two best friends.

When Mum handed over the parental consent forms for me, Nydia and Anne-Marie, she mentioned that she'd signed the forms on behalf of Anne-Marie and Nydia's parents. Then they asked her for a letter from both sets of parents giving her the authority to sign the forms and of course Mum didn't have one. Mum phoned Nydia's parents and they faxed through consent straightaway and spoke to Christina Darcy on the phone, so Nydia was fine. But we couldn't get hold of either one of Anne-Marie's parents. Anne-Marie tried phoning them, Mum tried and even the studio called their offices, but the best we could do was leave messages.

"Couldn't she start the audition process?" Mum asked Christina, her arms around Anne-Marie's shoulders.

"So she won't have to make up time once we get through to her mum and dad?"

"I'm sorry, Mrs Parker," Christina Darcy said. "It's the conditions of insurance. We can't advance with Anne-Marie until we have the correct paperwork."

"Typical, this is typical!" Anne-Marie had said, but not in a stroppy way. She spoke in a small, shaky voice, the sort that might cry at any minute.

"I'll keep trying," Mum promised, clutching her phone. "I'll try your dad's office here. I'm sure they'll be able to get a call to him."

"Yes, because he's bound to pick up the phone to his secretary," Anne-Marie said unhappily. "It's just his daughter he ignores."

"Everybody listen, please," Christina Darcy called out to the fifty or so of us in the holding room. "You will be called out in alphabetical order, by surname. Please have your sheet music ready. Remember – smile, relax, be yourself. OK?" We all murmured our assent.

"Good – Alexis Ackerman? Come through, please."

"I must be next," Nydia said anxiously, clutching her sheet music. "I feel nervous."

"At least it will be over with," I reassured her. "The trouble with being a P is that you are just enough along to be in the middle bit where they forget you, and not near enough the end to be memorable."

"Well, at least you are getting to do it!" Anne-Marie snapped. She looked over at my mum who was still on the phone, but I could tell by the look on Mum's face that she hadn't managed to track down one of Anne-Marie's parents yet.

Mum still hadn't got hold of them when it was finally my turn to go in. The room that had been full of chatting, buzzing kids had dwindled down to about ten, including me and Anne-Marie, because as soon as you'd had your chat and sung your song, you were taken off to wait in another room. I don't know if that was so the ones going in last wouldn't have an unfair advantage or just so the others couldn't tell us how scary it had been and make us run a mile. But either way, when there were only a few of us left, it was impossible for me not to talk to Kirsty O'Brien.

We hadn't spoken so far that morning, even though I knew she'd seen me and I knew that she knew I'd seen her. We'd glanced at each other and spent a lot of time trying not to look like we'd noticed each other – now it was impossible.

"Oh, hi!" I said as if I'd just spotted her. It made me look and feel like an idiot, but at least it gave us an excuse to start talking.

"Hi there!" Kirsty looked just as fake-surprised as me. We both laughed and smiled at each other.

"So you're in next?" I asked her. She nodded.

"I'm terrified," she grinned and her eyes sparkled. She was really pretty, but in a nice friendly way. The sort of way that made you think she'd be nice to be friends with if she wasn't on the verge of dating your ex-boyfriend.

"Well, break a leg," I said. "I'm sure you'll be fine."

"Is she OK?" Kirsty nodded over to where Anne-Marie was sitting, her head resting on my mum's shoulder as Mum talked on the phone.

"Parent problems," I told Kirsty. "Or lack of parent problems. She's got no one to sign her form."

"That sucks," Kirsty said. "My mom and dad are divorced, but I think they're more cool now than they were when they were married."

"Me too!" I said.

"Kirsty O'Brien!" Christina Darcy called out Kirsty's name.

"I'd better go," she said. "Keep your fingers crossed for me."

"I will, Kirsty," I said, watching her go. No wonder Danny liked her. I tried to imagine what I would feel like inside if I saw Danny Harvey and Kirsty O'Brien holding hands. But I didn't seem to feel anything; not cross or sad or jealous at all. I decided it had to be because of all the confusing and complicated things that were happening at the moment. My poor brain could probably only stand thinking about so many things, and Sean and his dad and Anne-Marie had got it working at full capacity. If my brain didn't want to deal with the idea of Danny and a new girlfriend I was OK with that.

"Oh *no!*" I heard Anne-Marie sob, just before she ran off towards the toilets.

"What's up?" I hurried over to Mum.

"Her dad's out of reach – on some mountain where there's only a satellite phone that doesn't seem to be working. And her mum is in China, so nowhere near LA at all. I don't know why she told that poor child she'd visit her here. Apparently she's in the middle of organising a show. Her assistant told me she was not to be disturbed unless someone was seriously ill or dead. I told the girl the circumstances, but she said interrupting her boss would get her the sack..." Mum trailed off, looking exasperated. "If I was in China I'd *interrupt* that woman. I'd *interrupt* her and ask why she'd bothered to have a child!"

I tried to think of something to say, but I couldn't think of anything. I'd always known that Anne-Marie's parents were hard to get hold of, but I'd always assumed that if she really needed them they'd be there. But they weren't. I couldn't imagine how she must feel.

"I'd better go and see if she's OK," I said. But before I could Christina Darcy called out my name.

"Ruby Parker!" I froze to the spot and looked at Mum.

"Go on, darling, you have to go," she said.

"But Anne-Marie...?" I looked over to where the toilets were.

"I'll go," Mum said.

"Ruby Parker!" Christina Darcy looked right at me.

"Go on, good luck," Mum urged me.

It felt wrong leaving Anne-Marie on her own in the loo when she was having such a terrible day. As I walked towards Christina Darcy, who was standing in the doorway of the rehearsal room frowning at me, I wondered if *I* was a terrible person. What sort of person put an audition before a friend and hid Sean's secret from everyone, not to mention having funny feelings about him when Anne-Marie was supposed to be his girlfriend. I supposed that I had to be a bad person. I had to be a *terrible* person, because a good person would not have left their friend crying all alone in the loo.

I walked into the studio feeling really bad, and worse still when I saw who was sitting on the panel alongside the directors and casting people. It was Sean. He smiled at me and I thought about what he'd said the night before by the pool, the fluttery feeling I got in my chest when I looked at him, and Anne-Marie in the toilets feeling so let down and alone.

"Can you hand your sheet music to the pianist, please, Ruby," Ralph Fearson, who was to be the film's director, said. I stood there holding 'Good Morning Baltimore' in my hands, frozen to the spot.

"Ruby?" Mr Fearson repeated.

"Rubes – are you OK?" Sean asked me with concern.

"No," I told Sean. "Anne-Marie is crying in the toilets because her parents aren't around to sign the consent form and she knows that if she doesn't audition today she'll lose her chance of being in the film."

"That's sad, but it's not your problem," Christina Darcy told me. "We've all tried to get through to her parents. They're simply not available. Our insurance won't let us audition her without the proper paperwork."

"So you see, Ruby, there's nothing you can do to help," Mr Fearson said, quite kindly.

"I know she can't audition without the right bits of paper," I said, hearing my voice as if another much more rebellious person was speaking. "But I could go to her and try to make her feel better. You could let me do that."

"Ruby." This time Mr Fearson sounded much less

kind. "If you walk out of here now you will be blowing your chance to be in this movie."

"Only if that's what you want," I said. I couldn't believe what I was saying, but somehow I couldn't stop myself. "After all, isn't *Spotlight!* all about friendship and loyalty? Isn't Arial exactly the sort of person who'd give up the spotlight and the stage for her friends, especially if they were in trouble. If I go to Anne-Marie now I'm showing you that I can be just as brave as Arial, just as determined and have enough belief in myself to know that the whole world's not going to fall to pieces if you tell me to go home. Which you might do after you hear me singing anyway as I only started rehearsing last night and my mum really can't play the piano."

As I finished speaking I clapped my hands over my mouth. It was as if I'd been possessed by the spirit of a much braver and probably more stupid girl.

Christina Darcy and Ralph Fearson looked at each other. Christina raised one eyebrow in an expression that could have either meant "execute her now" or "the girl's got guts". I didn't hold out much hope for the latter.

"What do you think, Sean?" Ralph asked him.

"Ruby's right," Sean said, gazing at me in a way that made me feel like my knees might dissolve. "And I think she's already shown us more of Arial than any actress we've seen so far."

Ralph shrugged. "OK, Ruby, you have fifteen minutes. But just so you know, it wasn't your heroic little speech that got you that time, it was our leading man's admiration. What Sean wants Sean gets. Now go and don't be late back."

"Thank you," I said, racing to the door.

"Oh and by the way...?"

I stopped and looked back at Mr Fearson.

"If you sing half as well as you talk, you could be our Arial."

When I got to the toilets, Mum was outside a cubicle. "Ruby! What are you doing here?" she asked, concerned.

"I said I had to come and see Anne-Marie," I told her, then spoke at the cubicle door. "Annie? I've only got fifteen minutes. Open up, come and talk to me. Mum's going to wait outside, aren't you, Mum?"

"Am I?" Mum asked. I scowled at her. "I mean, yes, I am. I'll be outside, love."

"She's gone," I called as the loo door swung shut. After a couple of seconds the cubicle door opened and Anne-Marie came out. Her eyes were puffy, swollen and red. Her nose was running and her face was streaked with tears. She peered at her reflection in the mirror.

"I look a sight," she said, sniffing and rubbing her eyes.

"I can't believe this has happened," I said, putting an arm around her. "It's so unfair."

"I know," Anne-Marie said, splashing her face with cold water. "I know it's unfair. But I *can* believe it, that's the problem. I go on every day as if it doesn't really matter that I never see my parents, as if it's all a bit of a joke that I have my own credit card and can do almost anything I like. Then something like this happens... and this is bad, Ruby. This is gut-wrenchingly awful. But what if I really *did* need them? What if it was a matter of life or death? Would they be there for me then?"

"Of course they would," I said, hugging her close as she burst into tears again.

"Are you sure? Because I'm not," Anne-Marie sobbed into my neck. "Sometimes I feel so alone and then I remember I've got friends like you. Friends who will walk out of a really important audition to see how I am, and I realise that I *am* lucky after all. I'd have never left an audition for you, you know."

"That's because you're not stupid," I said, wondering what Anne-Marie would think if she knew all the facts. "Wash your face and put some lipgloss on," I told her. "I don't think this is over for you after all. Know why? Because Sean is sitting in on the auditions too. And I heard that Sean gets what Sean wants. All you have to do is ask him to rearrange an audition for you after you've got hold of your parents and he will."

"No," Anne-Marie shook her head. "I can't do that."

"What? But why?" I asked her.

"Because I wanted to do this on my own," Anne-Marie said. "I know I was going on earlier about how me and Sean would have chemistry and that he could put in a word for me – but I also know Sean. I know he'd never do that. I knew that if I got a part in *Spotlight!* it would be down to me and not Sean. Even if he did make a fuss and get me another audition I'd always know that I'd needed help and I don't want to do that. I want to achieve things on my own merit."

"Annie." I put the back of my hand on her forehead. "Have you got a temperature?"

Anne-Marie laughed and batted my hand away. "I'm not quite as shallow as everyone thinks, you know," she told me.

"I know that better than anyone," I said.

"Well, your fifteen minutes is almost up. You'd better get back," Anne-Marie said. "I'll see you at the end of the day."

"Keep the faith," I told her as we walked out of the room.

"And you break a leg!" Anne-Marie called after me as I raced back to the rehearsal room. Looking back I sort of wish I had broken an actual leg. A spell in hospital would have kept me from getting myself into the most trouble ever.

It was hard to get my mind back on the workshops, but in the end I got carried way by the characters I was playing. I used all of the confusing thoughts and feelings that were whirling around in my head about Sean, Anne-Marie and everything, and tried to turn them into the way my characters might be thinking and feeling.

In the workshops we were separated into groups that the directors had picked. I had hoped to be in one with Nydia, but that didn't work out. As I glanced around at my group it didn't take me long to see that not only was I in Kirsty O'Brien's group I was also in Henry Dufault's. I didn't know quite what to make of this. Kirsty was obviously Arial material, so the fact that I was in a group with her made it quite likely they didn't think that I had a real shot at the lead. On the other hand, since I'd first met him I'd found out that Henry Dufault was a known troublemaker and wild card, who was talented but nearly impossible to control. He'd been fired from more jobs than I'd ever had, and yet directors and casting agents kept giving him chance after chance, so he had to be good. I would have thought they'd have put him in the group with the least hopeful candidates. I worried that my outburst that morning had got me marked as a troublemaker too, but that didn't apply to Kirsty or any of the other kids as far as I could see. In the end I decided not to think about it. I just got on with the tasks we were given.

We did some scenes from *Spotlight!*, each time swapping parts. We also did some scenes from other plays or films, some songs from various musicals and finally we were taught a dance routine. I was surprised at how good Henry was. I'd expected him to backchat and make smart comments, but he was really amazing. He literally acted the other kids off the floor. This made me think he wasn't sticking to the rules and so when it came to my turn to rehearse a scene to act with him, me as Arial and him as Sebastian, I was surprised when he treated me to a wicked grin.

"Ruby Parker," he said. "Finally someone I can mix it up with."

"What does that mean?" I asked him suspiciously.

"It means that everyone else in this group is a lame

duck," Henry told me. "I had to play it straight with them. But you know what you're doing – we can have some fun."

"I don't want to have fun," I said. "I want to learn my lines and say them and look like I mean it."

"OK, well you can learn Arial's lines if you like," Henry said. "But I'll be improvising."

"You're crazy," I whispered urgently to him. "You'll get us both kicked out."

"Or we'll impress them so much they'll give us parts."

"Don't be ridiculous," I said crossly. This seemed to make Henry laugh for some reason.

"I love English chicks," he told me. "You are all so uptight."

"Look, Henry, we're going to learn these lines as they are written in this script and when it's finally our time to perform, we're going to say them. Don't mess this up for me just because you don't care what happens." A few other kids looked over at us and I struggled to keep my voice down.

Henry smiled a long slow smile at me that made me feel even crosser. "I like you, Ruby Parker," he said. "You're feisty."

"Feisty!" I barked out a laugh. "I am not feisty. I am just a girl who wants to get a part in a film. I'm not feisty or uptight or a *chick* or anything. I've had a really bad day and you aren't making it any better. So let's get on with it, shall we?"

Henry bowed in the most irritatingly pretentious way and said, "Your wish is my command, my lady."

Of course when we came to perform our scene in front of all the important people, including Ralph Fearson, Christina Darcy and Sean Rivers, Henry didn't use one single line from the script. He improvised the whole thing. For about five seconds I tried to say my lines no matter what he said, but then I realised that would just make me look even more stupid. So I listened and reacted to what he said, and he listened and reacted to what I said. Somehow, by the end of our scene, we had more or less covered the same ground as the scene that had been written, except that instead of chewing pencils and looking at their clipboards and watches, Ralph and Christina were watching and listening closely to us. And I knew that I'd acted a hundred times better Henry's way than I would have if I'd just recited the lines. As we finished our group applauded us, even if the grown-ups didn't.

"Mr Dufault, Miss Parker – you don't feel the need for scriptwriters then?" Mr Fearson asked us.

"We do, sir, we certainly do," Henry said very politely.

"But we knew you'd heard that scene a hundred times over today so we thought we'd freshen it up for you."

"Improvisation is not a requirement for the cast in this film, Mr Dufault," Ralph Fearson said. "Concentration, ability to take direction and learn scripts *are*."

"And what about being able to act?" I heard this girl's voice say a few seconds before I realised it was mine. *My* voice coming out of *my* mouth. "Because we acted every single other kid off the stage just then. And yes, we can take direction and learn lines – I'll recite the whole scene for you now if you like. But more important than any of that, we can live inside the characters. We don't need a script to be the characters."

The others in our group, including Kirsty O'Brien, took a sharp inward breath. Henry Dufault looked at me full of admiration and I noticed Sean clapping all by himself as he leant against the wall.

What was wrong with me? It seemed that my overworked brain couldn't stand any more. It was determined to get me sacked so that I could leave Hollywood, go home and watch *Hollyoaks* for all eternity. Still I'd gone and said all of the rebellious words now, so there was no point in being miserable about it. I lifted my chin, pulled my shoulders back and waited to be sent home.

But all Ralph Fearson did was look at me very hard, drawing two very bushy brows together before writing something down on his notepad.

"OK, let's move on. Sean's here to act a scene with a couple of the girls. As you will all know by now, Sean Rivers has agreed to accept the role of Sebastian, which we are delighted about. It's crucial to find him the right Arial, so he's going to act the kiss scene with... Kirsty O'Brien and Ruby Parker."

Several things happened to me at once. First of all, after feeling nothing but really rather friendly towards Kirsty, I suddenly became extremely jealous of her. Second I realised that I would have to kiss Sean on the lips, and even though I knew it was a stage kiss and didn't mean anything, it would mean *everything* and I would immediately explode and die on the spot. And third, I realised that only Kirsty and I had been chosen out of all of the girls in the group to make out... I mean *try* out with Sean. I was cross, terrified and excited all at once.

"So you should know the song and the lines," Christina told us. "Kirsty, you're up first. Take your positions, please. And action!"

I sat and watched as sweet, pretty, nice Kirsty O'Brien made eyes at Sean while they sang together. I don't think that I'd ever heard Sean really singing before. Of course he had a great voice, and when he looked at Kirsty O'Brien, he really did look as if he loved her. I could tell that she felt it too because her cheeks went bright red. *It doesn't mean anything,* I told myself as 'Starlight Girl' came to an end and they kissed. I remembered when I'd been so worried about kissing Justin de Souza, back when I used to be in *Kensington Heights*. I used to have a silly crush on Justin too and I'd got really, really worried about my first stage kiss –my first *ever* kiss of any kind! In the end though, when it came right down to it, it was just like kissing a bit of cardboard. I'd felt nothing at all. So I was hopeful that's what it would be like with Sean too. After all, just because he was fabulously handsome and had recently told me he wished I was his girlfriend, and, oh, I seemed to be IN LOVE WITH HIM, why should it be any different? It was going to be fine.

"Ruby, you're up," Christina called over the applause of the group as she scribbled in her notebook.

I took a breath and looked at Sean. But instead of seeing him, I saw Sebastian, and instead of being me, Ruby Parker, the girl who gets herself into serious trouble, I was Arial, and everything was fine. I remembered all the lines, sang the song pretty nicely and was just gazing into Sebastian's eyes, preparing to kiss him, when suddenly he wasn't Sebastian any more, he was Sean.

My heart pounded, my tummy lurched and I forgot what I was supposed to say or do. All I could do was stare at him.

Sean sensed my hesitation and, smiling, leant towards me for the kiss, but I put my hand on his chest and pushed him back. Then, holding my gaze, Sean put one hand over mine and pulled me closer to him, whispering so quietly that no one but me could hear. "Don't worry, Ruby, this isn't me kissing you. It's Sebastian."

Then I felt the brush of his lips on mine for a moment and in a second the kiss was over.

The group was applauding again and Ralph and Christina were whispering in each other's ears.

"You're still holding my hand," I told Sean, snatching it back. "And looking at me – you're still looking at me."

"I was thinking," Sean said very quietly. "How amazing you are."

"Right then!" Christina bellowed, breaking the moment into a thousand pieces. "We've finished for today. The procedure is the same as before. We'll be calling your parents tonight to let them know if we want to see you again. Thanks for all of your hard work, and good luck! You can find your friends and parents in the lobby. Please don't leave until your parent or guardian has signed you out."

The lobby was noisy and crowded, full of excited kids and their families. I spotted Mum and Anne-Marie over the far side of the room, and I could see Nydia making her way towards them. But before I could join them I felt a hand on my wrist. I turned around and found Sean.

"I need to talk to you," Sean said.

"OK, at the house," I said.

"No, now, before we go back. I need to explain some things," Sean said. "Mum's not here with the car yet. It will only take a couple of minutes. Please?"

I glanced over at where Anne-Marie, Nydia and Mum were now all together on the other side of the large room.

"OK," I said, and I let Sean lead me a little way down an empty corridor that ran off the lobby.

"I don't want us to fall out," Sean said when we were more or less alone.

"Me neither," I said.

"I'm sorry I've freaked you out, what with my dad and all those things I said last night."

"Thanks," I said. "Because you have freaked me out a LOT, Sean. And it doesn't have to be like this. All you have to do is tell your mum about your dad, tell your dad you don't want the lead role in *Spotlight!* and tell Anne-Marie everything. Apart from that bit when you said you liked me. Don't tell her that whatever you do."

"But I do like you, Ruby," Sean said.

"Sean, no, you don't," I told him.

"And I think if it wasn't for Anne-Marie you'd like me too," Sean repeated. "Wouldn't you?"

I stared at him and thought of a hundred ways to tell him that I didn't like him at all, but then all at once I felt tired out. Tired of fighting, rebelling, being feisty and, most of all, tired of lying.

"OK! OK!" I said, taking a step back. "OK yes, Sean, I do like you. I don't know why now, after we've known each other for so long – but yes, I do, I do fancy you!"

"Ruby!"

I turned my head slowly to the side and saw Nydia and Anne-Marie staring at me and Sean. "Wait, it's not what it looks like—" I began.

"I'm going to—" Anne-Marie launched herself at me, but was caught by Nydia, who was looking at me as if I were the most disgusting thing she had ever seen.

"No, wait," I pleaded, holding out my upturned palms. "I was just about to tell Sean that it doesn't matter how I feel, I would never, ever do anything about it because you are my *friend*..."

"You're *dead*!" Anne-Marie hissed at me. "All this time I thought you were such a good friend and you were making moves on my boyfriend!"

"No, I wasn't...."

"She wasn't," Sean said. He looked at Anne-Marie. "I know you don't need to know this right now, but this isn't fair on Ruby. She wasn't chasing me. I was chasing her. I like her, Anne-Marie."

"You...?" Anne-Marie stared at Sean for a second. Then, her face bright red, she turned and fled back into the crowd.

Nydia marched up to me. I had never seen her so angry. "I *knew* something was going on yesterday," she said. "Ruby! How could you?"

"I couldn't! I haven't! I don't!" I tried to reassure her.

"You *never* treat a best friend this way," Nydia said shaking her head. "You never treat another girl this way. I'm through with you, Ruby."

As she walked away I stared at Sean. "Look what you've done," I said. "You've made things a hundred times worse."

"I'm sorry, Ruby, I was trying to help."

I shook my head. "Now you and I have to go and

find Mum and Nydia and Anne-Marie, and wait for your mum to pick us up. And then we all have to drive home together. And thanks to you, I don't have my two best friends any more."

"You've got me," Sean said with a miserable half-smile.

I scowled at him. "Yes," I said. "That's the problem."

Ruby

Just to make things clear, we are not speaking to you any more. We aren't friends any more either. We'll be polite to you in front of your mum and at the studio, but we both think that you are a horrible person. We aren't speaking to Sean either.

Nydia and Anne-Marie

Chapter Ten

I found the folded note on my pillow when I went up to my room after we got back from the studio. At least I assume it started out life on my pillow. When I found it, David had it firmly clenched between his paws and was chewing enthusiastically on the corner. I don't know how Nydia got it there so quickly. She and Anne-Marie must have written it in the car while I wasn't looking, which wouldn't have been that hard because I spent the whole time staring out of the window wishing I could magic myself back an hour and change everything. However no amount of wishing changed anything (I am starting to learn that hardly ever happens) and there the note was. A few lines on a bit of paper that confirmed my two best friends hated me.

I couldn't blame them, *I* hated me. After all, even if I hadn't exactly gone after Sean I'd thought about him and had funny feelings about him. Plus I hadn't told anyone about his secret meetings with his dad, which I was fairly sure were a really bad idea.

Just at that moment there was a quiet knock on the door. I hoped it was Nydia coming to say that they'd thought it over and they wanted to make up.

"Come in?" I said nervously.

It was Sean.

"Go away," I hissed furiously.

"I am, I am going away," Sean said. "I'm going out to meet Dad for a burger. I've told Mom I'm having an early night. If she finds out I'm not in bed and asks, will you say that I'm out with Danny?"

"Haven't you got me into enough trouble today?" I asked him, exasperated.

Sean's look was pleading. "Please, Ruby, things are going really great with Dad. We're getting on so much better. I'm nearly ready to tell Mom. I just need to make sure that we're really OK first."

I shook my head. "He's your dad, Sean – you shouldn't have to make sure whether or not he's OK with you. He should just be OK with you whatever – whether you're a film star or not. Talking of which, when are you going to tell the studio that you don't want to play Sebastian?"

"Really soon," Sean said. "I just need a bit longer with Dad. Honestly it's different now, Ruby, and he's so pleased that I've taken the part. I don't want to let him down."

"Of course he's pleased! He thinks you're going to make him millions of dollars again – it's not because he loves you or cares about you," I snapped before I could shut my mouth. "Sean... I'm sorry, I'm just really worried about you."

"That's not true," he said quietly. "Dad really cares about me."

"I hope so," I said, hugging my pillow hard. "Look, go. I'll cover for you, OK?"

And then everything that happened that day hit me like a ton of bricks and I cried and cried. I just couldn't believe that my best friends really hated me and that everything was going so wrong when it should have been feeling so right. Maybe it was Hollywood. Maybe I would always be miserable here.

"Ruby?"

I must have fallen asleep because the next thing I remember was my mum's voice gently calling me. "Ruby, wake up, love."

I rolled over and pushed my hair out of my eyes, squinting at her.

"You've been crying," Mum said with concern. "Anne-Marie is still very upset too. She and Nydia have been out by the pool in a huddle since we got back. Why are you stuck up here? Is everything OK?"

I sighed and wished I could tell my mum the real reason I was upset, but when I thought about it there wasn't a single thing on my list that she would either understand or be able to fix. She wouldn't get why Sean had to see his dad in secret and lie to his mum about everything, including wanting to be Sebastian in *Spotlight!* And she wouldn't understand that Nydia, Anne-Marie and I had fallen out because they thought I was trying to go out with Sean even though I wasn't, even though I did like him. So although I'd promised that now I'd always tell my mum everything, I decided not to tell her this. After all, there was nothing she could do and she would only worry.

"I'm just tired," I said. "It's been a really, really long day."

Mum smiled and hugged me. "I know. Sean's already asleep, poor lad, and it's going to be another long day tomorrow! They've called you back for the final round of auditions!"

"Really?" I sat up, feeling almost happy for a second. Then I remembered that everybody hated me and I was all alone and I lay down again.

"What about Nydia?" I asked.

"Yes, Nydia too," Mum told me. "Ruby, you are really close to being in a Hollywood movie again."

I nodded thoughtfully and Mum must have been able to see the worry in my face.

"Listen, Ruby," she said, putting her hand over mine. "Are you ready for this? Because if it's all too much pressure I'll understand. You know that this film is going to be massive. And if you get a part you won't just be Ruby Parker girl/actress/singer any more. You'll be Ruby Parker Superstar."

I looked up at my ceiling and tried to imagine what that would mean. It still seemed so impossible and far away that I couldn't really understand it. And despite everything that had happened today, I knew I still wanted the part of Arial. I knew I wanted it even though Nydia really wanted it too. It was the best thing happening to me at the moment and I wasn't going to give up trying to get it.

"I'm ready," I said firmly. "Besides I know that whatever happens, and even if one day I win an Oscar, you'll always make sure that I'm still just Ruby Parker girl."

"That's true," Mum said. "Do you want to come down for something to eat?"

I shook my head. "I'm going to go back to sleep," I yawned.

"I'll bring you up a sandwich." Mum never believed that I wasn't hungry and she was usually right.

"Listen, Ruby, I'm sure you'll make up with Anne-Marie and Nydia soon. I've never known you three to be apart for too long. And as far as Sean is concerned I know you'll do the right thing, you always do. And you can talk to me you know I was young once – I can still just about remember being your age if I concentrate really, *really* hard."

I was speechless as Mum kissed me on the forehead and walked out of the door. Even when I didn't tell her anything, she still knew everything. Freaky.

I was full up with toasted cheese sandwiches and fast asleep when I was woken by tapping at my window. I lay there for a moment in the dark, trying to work out what was going on. David must have crept on to my bed while I was asleep because he sprang into life at my side and bared his teeth at the window.

It was a full moon outside and the sky was a light orange colour because of the millions of city lights that blazed in the valley, but even so I was scared as David and I tiptoed towards the window, him growling and trembling all at once. Cautiously I opened it and peeped out. A stone about the side of a large raisin hit me on the cheek.

"Ouch!" I said loudly, before remembering I was scared.

"Ruby, it's me." I peered over the sill and saw Sean standing in the shadows. "It's later than I thought and the door's locked. I'm guessing that Mom hasn't missed me, but it looks like everyone is asleep and I can't get in without tripping the alarm."

"Everyone is asleep, except me apparently," I said testily.

"Can you sneak down and let me in?" Sean whispered.

"Can't you just climb up a drain pipe," I hissed back.

"There are no drain pipes," Sean told me. "Please, Ruby, or I'll have to stay out here all night and come up with an elaborate sleepwalking story."

"That works for me," I said. I was about to pull my head in and slam the window when I realised that I couldn't do that to a friend, even if just at the moment he was a particularly irritating one. "Go round to the front," I told him.

I had to shut David in my room because I knew that he'd get all excited by a midnight adventure and start barking, which would wake the whole house up. He had a surprisingly loud bark for such a small dog. He whimpered a bit as I closed the door on him, but I knew that after a couple of seconds he'd get back into bed and curl up on the warm spot that I had just left.

The house was quiet; I looked at Jeremy's grandfather clock that stood at the top of the stairs. It was past midnight – Sean really had stayed out late. I thought about the last time I had snuck down the stairs when I was "borrowing" my mum's credit card to pay for my secret flight back to London. It had been much riskier then – Mum and Jeremy had been up and sitting only a few metres way from me as I crawled to delve into her handbag. But even though everyone in the house was fast asleep I felt much more scared this time. Maybe because I knew that Sean was on the other side of the door.

"Thanks," Sean said as I unlatched the door and quickly reset the alarm.

"That's OK," I whispered. "Night then."

"Ruby, stay a while...?" Sean asked.

"Stay? Why?"

"Come through to the kitchen," Sean said. "We can have a midnight snack."

"I'm not hungry," I lied. But the cheese toasties hadn't filled me up and the sound of my tummy rumbling was almost louder than the burglar alarm would have been.

"Come on, I can hear that from here," Sean joked. Furiously I followed him. Anyway I really fancied some cereal.

"So how was it?" I asked him as he passed me the milk and I sloshed it on to my Cheerios.

"It was great, really great!" Sean was bright eyed and happy. "We had a burger and then we went bowling. And Dad said he was so proud of me and how much he missed me."

"Really," I said. "And did you tell him that you were ready to pull out of the film? You know, before they start shooting it and wasting hundreds of millions of dollars."

"He said that I hadn't signed a contract yet, and that as long as I hadn't I can do what I like. He even said he'd read the contract for me if I wanted."

"Did he mention your reputation?" I asked him. "Sean, maybe you don't want to be a film star now, but one day you might change your mind – and then everyone's going to wonder if you'll pull out at the last minute again."

"I hadn't thought of that," Sean said, looking worried.

"No, and I don't think your dad has either," I said. "I think he thinks you won't pull out of the film at all."

"Well, maybe I won't," Sean said defiantly.

"Great!" I exclaimed. "But why? Because it's what you want, or because it's what your dad wants?"

"I've really enjoyed the last few days," Sean told me. "And I *really* enjoyed acting with you today. We don't get to do that enough."

"Yes, well," I said, suddenly finding my Cheerios extremely interesting.

"Look," Sean slid a little closer to me on the counter. "I know now is not a good time for you and me. I know we have a million other things we have to deal with, but hopefully one day that will change. I hope you will still like me then, because I know I'll still like you."

I made myself look into his blue eyes and for just a second it seemed like a terribly good idea to kiss him. Then Anne-Marie turned up at the kitchen door.

"How sweet," she said, crossing her arms. "Is this where you have your secret meetings? No wonder you're looking so rough, Ruby; you're not getting enough sleep."

"Anne-Marie – there is nothing going on between me and Sean," I tried explaining.

"Yes, it looks like it," she replied sharply. "Apart from the whole having your lips two millimetres apart thing."

"That was..." I struggled. "That did look bad, but please, Annie, I would never, *ever* go behind your back with your boyfriend. I wouldn't do that!"

Anne-Marie shook her head. "Don't call me Annie," she said. She went to the fridge and poured herself a glass of juice. "I'll be out of your hair soon. I finally got through to Dad this evening. It turns out that he's going to be in LA tomorrow and then he's flying to London for two days. I'm going back with him. There's no point in me being here any more."

"Can't your dad talk to the studio, get them to give you another chance?" I asked Anne-Marie. After all her dad was a famous movie producer.

Anne-Marie took a swig of her juice. "He could, but like I told you earlier today, back when I thought you actually cared about what I felt, I don't want any special favours. And besides this is the last place I want to be."

"Annie," Sean began. "Let's talk about this."

"I said, don't call me Annie!" Anne-Marie snapped, with tears brimming in her eyes, and she ran off back upstairs.

"We suck," I said, miserably pushing the bowl of Cheerios away from me.

"You don't," Sean said. "I do. All of this is my fault."

"I wish it was," I said, looking at him. "But it's a bit me too. Sean, I can't go out with you now or probably ever. Not if I want to get my friends back, and I *do*. I *need* my friends."

"OK," Sean said sadly. "But we're still friends too, aren't we?"

"Of course," I said. "Although not for much longer if you keep making me get up in the middle of the night to let you in."

Chapter Eleven

We found out there were only about ten kids left auditioning when we arrived at the studio. I didn't recognise any of the others except for Henry Dufault. Nydia smiled and nodded at a couple and so did Kirsty. They must have been in the other groups yesterday with them.

Christina Darcy and Ralph Fearson had appeared along with Sean to speak to us all.

"Well, you are our final choices for the lead roles. As you know there are four leads. Sean is already cast as Sebastian so it's the other three we need to finalise. We've decided who is suited to which role and you will only be able to audition for that role now. Today it's all about your screen presence, your chemistry with Sean and your acting ability. So just enjoy it, immerse yourself in the characters and don't mess up."

"So no pressure then," Henry whispered in my ear. I found myself nodding in agreement, but then caught

Christina Darcy watching me, so I came to my senses and remembered that I found Henry really quite annoying.

"Ruby, Nydia and Kirsty – we want you to audition for the part of Arial. Follow me, please." I heard a sharp intake of breath behind me from the other girls who realised their chance to play Arial was over for good.

As we followed Christina Darcy I smiled at Nydia. "We've made it this far – it's amazing, isn't it?" I said, forgetting she hated me.

"It is amazing," Nydia growled at me. "But I imagine Sean's secret girlfriend has a better chance than Kirsty or me."

"You're Sean's secret girlfriend?" Kirsty exclaimed, wide-eyed. "Cool!"

"No, I am *not*," I whispered, hoping Christina hadn't heard. "For the last time, I like Sean, Sean likes me, but we are *not* and never will be going out together!"

"I'd totally go out with Sean Rivers," Kirsty said. "Secretly or otherwise."

"I thought you were going out with Danny?" I asked her, diverted for a second.

"Well, kinda – only he hasn't actually asked me. We just hang out a lot."

"That's Danny for you, eh, Nydia?" I said. But Nydia blanked me.

"OK, if you don't believe me, your best friend of a hundred years, then that's fine," I said. "Good luck with your audition and may the best girl win."

"I intend to," Nydia said.

As she flounced off after Christina, followed closely by Kirsty, I stood stock still and stared. That wasn't Nydia, my all-for-one-and-one-for-all best friend. Even if I *had* secretly been going out with Sean behind Anne-Marie's back I wasn't sure I deserved that. And then I realised, maybe it wasn't just the thing that hadn't happened between me and Sean that had made Nydia suddenly so cross with me. Maybe it was *this*. Her and me battling for a part that we both really wanted. We'd never been in this situation before. Even when we all auditioned for the part of Polly Harris in *The Lost Treasure of King Arthur,* Nydia didn't get past the first round of auditions so we were never really in direct competition. Come to think of it, she had been a bit annoyed with me back then too, thinking that I'd got all stuck up just because I was making a movie. And when she'd gone on the TV talent show to find the lead for the UK version of *Spotlight!*, I'd given up show business and was really only in the chorus by mistake. I wasn't her competition then. And now here she was going for the same part as me (and Kirsty) and, as far as she was concerned, I was the leading man's secret girlfriend. No wonder she was furious with me.

I followed Nydia into the room where Sean, Ralph Fearson, Christina and Kirsty were waiting. I had a choice to make. Should I try and throw this audition and hope that they chose Nydia? Because if I did I was fairly sure I'd have my old friend back much more quickly, and pretty soon we'd be back home in London and all of this would be water under the bridge. Or should I do my best to try and win this part because I was good enough and I deserved it, and because I wanted it?

And then I realised there wasn't really a choice. I wasn't choosing between my best and oldest friend and my career. I was choosing to try my best or to not try at all – and that wasn't a choice I could make. I wanted to be Ruby Parker Superstar.

I had to give this audition everything. And let whatever was going to happen next happen.

At lunch time we were allowed to take our sandwiches outside to have at picnic tables that were arranged in a courtyard at the centre of the studio complex. Nydia went to sit with the girls she knew from her group and I went to sit on my own. It wasn't long before Kirsty joined me and I was glad to see her.

"Hey," she said, sliding along the bench next to me. "How do you think you're doing?"

I'd done quite a few scenes with Sean during the morning and I'd been relieved to find that it wasn't weird at all, even in the soppy romantic ones. Sean was such a good actor I knew that when he looked at me, he was seeing Arial, which helped to look at him and see Sebastian. Arial was allowed to stare dreamily into his electric blue eyes and hold his hand and feel romantic, and it wasn't confusing at all. OK, it was very confusing, but if I concentrated very hard I could just about get my head around the whole situation. I'd sat and watched as Kirsty and Nydia acted the same scenes with Sean and I had to admit I thought both of them were excellent. Later we were going to be screen-tested individually again and sing once more. After that, they'd make their decision.

"I think I'm doing my best. What about you?"

"Same," Kirsty said. "I'd like the role. It's going to be such a huge film."

"Yes, I know," I said. "Does that worry you? The pressure of fame at such a young age?"

Kirsty shook her head. " Truly? No. *The Young Robin Hood* is going to change my career for good and, besides,

I have cool parents who won't let me get carried away or work too much. No, there's really only one thing that worries me right now..."

"What's that?" I asked her.

"How can I get Danny to ask me out on a date?" Kirsty said.

I laughed so hard I nearly fell off the bench and all the people on Nydia's table looked over at us, except Nydia who scowled at her food.

"Don't ask me," I laughed. "Me and Danny never did things in the conventional way. We were always falling out or breaking up over something, and not telling each other when we didn't like each other and not telling each other when we did. But my advice is, if you like him then ask *him* out – because he's quite shy really plus very bad at saying what he's feeling."

"Me ask a guy out?" Kirsty looked shocked for a moment, but then she smiled. "Why didn't I think of that?"

"Ladies," Henry appeared from nowhere and grinned at us as he sat down. Then he winked at me which made me feel instantly cross, but I couldn't say anything because I had a mouth full of food.

"So I could ask you how your audition is going and all that," Henry said, "but I am a man of few words and I'd like to cut right to the chase. Ruby Parker, I dig you. Can I take you on a date?"

I looked at Kirsty, who was sitting open mouthed. "See Danny would never do *that,*" she said.

"Well, can I?" Henry persisted.

I couldn't answer him straightaway because I was chewing wholemeal bread and it was really quite seedy. Also I was slightly worried I might have some bits stuck in my teeth so I kept chewing for a bit longer than I needed to and tried to look as if I was just being thoughtful. Why on earth would I want to go on a date with a boy who I found irritating, annoying and seemed to bring out the worst in me whenever I was around him? No, there was no way I was going on a date with Henry Dufault.

But the words that came out of my mouth were, "OK then."

That was the other thing that happened whenever I was around Henry. I said things I absolutely never usually would. It was most inconvenient.

"Great, I'll call you later and arrange it." Henry winked at me again and I seethed.

"You don't have my number," I said.

"Ruby, I've so got your number," Henry said, and then he was gone.

"You are going on a date with Henry Dufault," Kirsty said.

"I know! How did that happen?" I dropped my head in my hands.

"Millions of girls across America would love to date Henry Dufault," Kirsty told me. "He's mad, bad and dangerous to know!"

"That's what I'm worried about," I said. "Why did I say yes? I didn't mean to say yes!"

Kirsty tipped her head on one side so that her blonde hair fell over one shoulder. "Maybe because you don't hate him at all," she suggested. "And maybe because whenever you are around him, you light up like a Christmas tree."

"Don't be so ridiculous," I said. "I have a doomed crush on Sean Rivers. I can't possibly like Henry Dufault."

"Are you sure you have a crush on Sean?" Kirsty asked me. "Or is it just easier to like someone you know you'll never be with?"

From: Danny (dharvey@breakaleg.co.uk)

To: Ruby (rparker@beverlyhills.com)

Subject: How are you?

Hi Rubes

Kirsty told me what happened with Nydia and Anne-Marie. I hope you don't mind. She wasn't doing it to be gossipy. She really likes you and she thought maybe you could do with a friend. I know you and me haven't been that close since the whole Auto-tune Miracle Microphone incident, but I hope you know that I will always be your friend. And I know that you and Sean wouldn't do anything behind Anne-Marie's back. I'm not surprised he likes you though. I've always thought he did.

Kirsty also said you're going on a date with Henry Dufault. Good luck with that!

Anyway, I know you find out tonight who's going to get the part of Arial. I can't say who I choose because all three of you are great – but good luck from me.

We're off to Romania to film in a couple of days, but if you can meet up for a milkshake or something before then let me know.

Your friend
Danny

Chapter Twelve

To say that the atmosphere in the house was a bit strained that evening was like saying that Jade Caruso was a BIT irritating. In other words, it was an understatement. So I was really pleased to see Danny's e-mail ping into my inbox. It was good to know that we were friends and that I didn't feel odd about him any more, not even though he knew about the thing that hadn't happened between me and Sean, and Henry asking me out on a date. I didn't mind that he didn't mind, and I didn't mind that he and Kirsty liked each other. It was official. I was over Danny Harvey. At last.

If only everything else was as simple. When we pulled up outside Jeremy's house, there was a big black limo parked on the drive and I guessed it was Anne-Marie's dad come to take her home. Nydia got out of the car first and went in before me and Mum, slamming the door behind her so it nearly took the tips of my fingers off.

"Still not made up yet?" Mum asked me. I shook my

head. "I expect it's the nerves." She patted me on the arm. "I'm sure that once we've had that phone call tonight and we know what's what, then everything will be all right between you." She glanced at the limo and pressed her lips together. "Right, I have a few things to say to Mr Chance."

But when we got indoors, it was pretty clear that Anne-Marie had said most of them already.

"I have a job, Anne-Marie," Mr Chance was saying as she stood with her hands on her hips in front of him. "An important job that keeps a roof over your head and pays your school fees. I let you have whatever you want; you have more freedom then any other child of your age that I know of. I am sorry I couldn't be there to sign this form in time, but that's the way it goes sometimes. You need luck on your side; it's all about breaks."

"Really? Funny that, because for a lot of fourteen-year-old girls all they need are their *parents* on their side. If I had just one parent who put me before work then none of this would have happened. I wasn't asking you to be with me, Dad. I gave up hoping for that when I was about five. All I needed was one signature."

There was a silence as Mr Chance and Anne-Marie glared at each other. I was proud of Anne-Marie, telling her dad how she really felt. It must have been hard when she hardly ever sees him. And he looked all shifty and stupid like the boys at school do when Mr Petrelli catches them mucking about with maracas.

"Listen, Anne-Marie, you are not being reasonable," Mr Chance said. He was wearing a white shirt and sunglasses pushed up on to his grey hair, a look that was far too young for him.

"Of course I'm not being reasonable!" Anne-Marie shouted back. "I've just lost out on the best audition ever, not because I wasn't good enough but because my parents couldn't be bothered to answer the phone!"

"If you'd found out exactly what was required beforehand..."

And then Anne-Marie flew at her dad, pummelling her fists into him. She was crying and he was just standing there, looking sort of bewildered and as if he'd rather be anywhere else in the entire world. What he should have done was to put his arms around her and hug her, but he didn't. Which is probably why, after the initial shock, my mum raced over. Mum wrapped her arms around Anne-Marie and hugged her tight, as she sobbed into Mum's hair. I wanted to go and hug her too, but I didn't think she'd want me to. So I just stood there, not wanting to leave, not wanting to look.

"This poor girl has had a very difficult time," Mum

told Mr Chance. "I don't think we've met before – I'm Janice Parker, the woman you entrusted your daughter's care to here in Hollywood."

I could hear the ice and anger in my mum's voice, but I don't think Mr Chance could. I think he was just relieved to have someone else there to manage his daughter so he didn't have to try and figure out what to do.

"Mrs Parker, I am so sorry for the inconvenience..." Mr Chance began, treating her to his smarmy smile.

"Anne-Marie is not an inconvenience," Mum snapped. "She's a lovely, funny, sweet girl – or don't you even know that about your daughter?"

It suddenly dawned on Mr Chance that my mum was fed up with him too. I don't think he was used to people standing up to him. He looked rather shocked.

"Well, anyway," he said stiffly. "What's done is done and it can't be changed. Life is hard and the sooner children learn that, the better they will do. Anne-Marie and I are booked on a flight out of LAX this evening. We need to get going..."

He looked at the back of Anne-Marie's head. "Are you packed, Anne-Marie?"

Anne-Marie pulled away from my mum and nodded without looking at him. "I'll go and get my bags," she said quietly. All the fire and anger had burnt out and drained away, and now she looked sad and small. I wasn't used to seeing her look that way and I was really upset that some of it might be because of me.

I watched as she ran up the stairs and then, after a second's hesitation, I followed. I had to try and talk to her.

She was zipping up her case when I walked in, stuffing in some of the new dresses and shoes she had bought and trying to lean on the lid of the case while zipping it up. She wasn't having much luck. I was glad to see that Nydia wasn't with her, but I was sure she'd turn up soon so I knew I'd better make it quick.

"Hi," I said. It wasn't my best ever start to a making-up speech.

"Hi," she sniffed without looking at me. But she didn't throw anything at me either and I took that as a good sign.

"I'm really sorry that you're so upset. I really hate to see you like this," I said tentatively. "And I know that part of the reason is because of what you think happened with me and Sean. Anne-Marie, I am so sorry. Are you still really angry with me?"

Anne-Marie looked up then and I could tell she must have been crying for a lot longer than when her dad got here.

"It's just that you *knew,* Ruby," she said. "I told you how important you and Sean were to me, especially with my rubbish parents, and all this time you were..."

"But we *weren't,*" I said. "Honestly, Anne-Marie. It wasn't even until we got to Hollywood that things went a bit bizarre. I've never fancied Sean before and he's never liked me..."

"He has, he always has," Anne-Marie said wearily. "And I've always known that, but you were with Danny. And anyway I never thought you'd really go out with him..."

"And you were right! Because I wouldn't!" I exclaimed. "I like Sean, I like him a lot – but *you*? You are one of my best friends and I *love* you."

Anne-Marie said nothing as she wrestled with her case. It kept pinging open no matter what she did to it. After another second's thought I went over and pressed my elbows down on the lid, squidging it flat. Bits of shoes and clothes poked out all around the edges.

"Quick," I said. "Jam your stuff in now and do up the zip!" I pressed my elbows down with all my might and Anne-Marie eased the zip round, stuffing in bits of stray fashion as she went until finally it was shut.

"Done!" she said, smiling for the first time.

"At last!" I said, standing up. We eyed the case suspiciously as if we both expected it to explode, but when it didn't, we half smiled at each other. "Anyway,"

I said, "it looks likes I'm going on a date with Henry Dufault."

"Really?" Anne-Marie looked sceptical. "But I thought you hated him?"

"I do," I said. "Or at least, I think I do, but I said I'd go, so I guess that point is up for debate."

"Does Sean know?" she asked.

"I don't think so," I said. "We haven't talked that much since yesterday. Look, the way he finished with you was really rubbish and he knows that. If you talk to him maybe you can sort things out before you leave?"

Anne-Marie shook her head and gave me a watery smile. "No," she said. "I'm not ready to talk to Sean. But it's nice to talk to you. Come and hug me."

"Does this mean we're still friends?" I asked her hopefully as I had my arms around her.

"I suppose," Anne-Marie said, sounding a little bit like herself. "You chose me over Sean and for any girl to do that must mean that she is usually a really good friend."

"Do you think you could tell Nydia that before you go?" I asked her as she hefted her case off the bed.

Anne-Marie shrugged. "Yeah, I'll tell her that we're OK. But you'll sort it out. You and Nydia never fall out. You are like the Great Wall of China."

"What? Do you mean really strong with deep foundations?" I asked, a bit perplexed.

"No you can both be seen from outer space," Anne-Marie said, and suddenly the old, fun, wise-cracking, sarcastic Anne-Marie was back. I knew she wasn't completely back; I knew she was still hurt and upset and confused, but I knew she was insulting me to prove that our friendship was on the mend and that meant a lot to me.

"I deserved that one," I said with a wry smile.

"I'll say," Anne-Marie said as she lugged her case into the hall. "And now I have a ten-hour flight with my dad to look forward to."

When we got downstairs, everyone was there to say goodbye to Anne-Marie, including Nydia and Sean. Anne-Marie hugged my mum hard, and then Mrs Rivers, and then she hugged me again, so that Nydia and Sean could see I suppose. Both of them looked fairly surprised.

"Bye, Nyds," she said, hugging her too. "Listen, I've had a chat to Ruby and we're cool now so don't feel you have to blank her over me. That would be even sillier than girls falling out over a boy."

"If you say so," Nydia said, glancing at me.

"Bye, Annie," Sean said as Anne-Marie walked past him. She paused and turned to look at him.

"You dumped me in the worst possible way at the worst possible time and I think you are pathetic," she said. "And if you ever call me Annie again I'll punch your pretty blue lights out. Got it?"

"Got it," Sean said.

I had hoped that after Anne-Marie had gone Nydia would come and find me so that we could make up, or that at least I'd be able to try and talk to her. But she went straight up to her room and shut the door, after asking Mum to call her if we heard any news.

But we didn't hear anything for ages. Time had never gone by so slowly, there had never been less on TV and the phone had never been so quiet before. So quiet in fact that I caught Mum picking it up just to check it had a dialling tone, which would have been funny except that I'd just done that exact same thing about five minutes before.

At some point I knew we would find out who would be playing the role of Arial. But the evening seemed to be going on for all eternity.

I wanted it to be me, but if it was, would I ever be friends with Nydia again? After all, she had been Arial in the UK TV special. She was really the most qualified of us of all to do it and she was more than good enough. If they picked me and not her I wasn't sure that we'd ever be friends again. But what if they picked her?

I tried to imagine how I would feel. I think it would be like when you see four actors on a split screen waiting to find out if they've won an award. They all have the same smile on their faces – a fake one. And when they hear a name being called out that isn't theirs, they keep on fake-smiling and usually nod as if to say they knew all along it wasn't going to be them that won the award and that they weren't bothered anyway, because awards are meaningless. But inside they are hurting really, really badly. That's how I would feel if they picked Nydia. I'd be glad for her, and glad that a girl who deserved the job had got it, but if it wasn't me I'd be gutted. I would feel as if my insides had been torn out and I was empty.

Of course it could be Kirsty O'Brien. If it was then I'd feel exactly the same only perhaps a little bit of relief. Because then me and Nydia would go back home to London together knowing neither one of us was better than the other.

That's when my mobile rang. I looked at it for a panicky moment, wondering if it was the studio calling me with the news as it was a local number I didn't recognise. But I was sure they'd said they were going to phone Mum direct. I was sure they wouldn't break news of this import direct to the child involved, because if it was bad news or anything I might jump out of a window or need counselling. If it was good news I might jump out of a window or need counselling. Knowing how worried the studio was about being sued, I was sure the call couldn't be from them. I seriously hoped not anyway. After a deep breath I pressed *answer* on my phone and held it to my ear.

"Hello?" I said uncertainly.

"Hi, Ruby, it's Kirsty." As I heard her voice I felt a strange mixture of relief and disappointment because I still didn't know anything – but then I thought, hang on, perhaps Kirsty knows. Perhaps they've already given Kirsty the part and she's rung to commiserate with me.

"I hope you don't mind me calling," Kirsty said. "Danny gave me your number because I was freaking out waiting for the phone to ring. He said I should talk to you because you were the best freaker-outer in show business and that after talking to you for five minutes I'd feel really sane."

"Oh, tell Danny thanks," I said sarcastically. "So you still haven't heard?"

"Nothing. I was wondering if you had."

"Nothing." But as I said it I heard the house phone ring downstairs. "Did you hear that?" I asked Kirsty, my voice tight.

"Yep," she said. "Is it them?"

"Hang on, I'll find out." Still with my mobile in my hand I went out of my bedroom door at exactly the same time as Nydia. We looked at each other and slowly walked down the stairs to the hallway where Mum has answered the phone. David, Sean, Sean's mum, Alberto and Marie were all standing there staring at my mum as she talked.

"Yes, Miss Darcy," Mum said, nodding. "Yes... uh-huh... uh-huh... yes, I see... I see... of course. Of course. Of course." Me and Nydia looked at each other, a temporary truce between as we waited to hear our fate. "Yes, yes, I'll explain everything," Mum said finally, her voice completely neutral. "Thank you so much. Goodbye."

She hung up and we all stared at her.

"Right," Mum said. "Ruby, Nydia – would you like to follow me into the study, please?"

As we followed I put my phone to my ear. "Still there?" I asked Kirsty.

"Yes, but now *my* phone is ringing. I'd better go," Kirsty said. "Call you later."

Nydia and I walked into Jeremy's study and sat on the brown leather sofa opposite his desk. Mum looked from me to Nydia and back again.

"Are you two still not talking?" she said, which

made both Nydia and I breathe out frustrated sighs. What did that have to do with *anything*?

"No, we're not," I said quickly. "But, Mum, what did Christina Darcy say? Who's got the part?"

Mum paused and pressed her lips into a thin line and knotted her fingers together. This usually meant that she was either cross or about to deliver a lecture. I suspected lecture. I just couldn't believe she had chosen now to give it!

"Acting is an extremely competitive career," Mum began, so off the topic that I wondered if she'd forgotten what we were supposed to be talking about. "People's feelings get hurt all the time. Ruby, you remember how you felt when those reviews for *The Lost Treasure of King Arthur* came out, don't you? All actors get rejected at one stage or another, even really good ones..."

"Are you saying we both got rejected?" I interrupted her. I love my mum, but sometimes she can really go on.

"No..." Mum paused as if debating what to say next. "In fact, one of you has got the part."

Nydia and I stared at each other and suddenly I realised that we were holding hands, gripping each other's fingers tightly.

"Who then? Who's got it?" Nydia squeaked.

“I’m not going to tell you,” Mum said steadily. “Not until you’ve cleared up your differences.”

“Mum!” “Mrs Parker!” Nydia and I wailed at the same time.

One of us had got the most hotly-contested part in the history of Hollywood teen musicals and only my mother knew which. So it was typical that she decided to use that power over Nydia and me to try and sort us out now.

“Look,” Mum said firmly, “if you two want to be actresses and go up for these big roles then you’ll find yourself competing against each other a lot. You need to make sure that your friendship survives, because one thing I’ve learnt is that a good friend should always be there for you, no matter what. And you should always be there for your friends. You mustn’t fall out over parts.”

“We haven’t fallen out over the part,” Nydia told Mum. “We fell out because Sean dumped Anne-Marie for Ruby, and Ruby says she would go out with Sean—”

“If he wasn’t Anne-Marie’s boyfriend!” I interrupted hotly. “And besides that’s *not* the reason why we’ve fallen out. Not really. I’ve talked to Anne-Marie. I’ve explained things to her, which is more than you’ll let me do. I think you’re angry with me because of this audition. You want the part of Arial. You want it really badly and you think you deserve it – and so do I. Me and Sean might have given you a reason to be angry with me. But this, *this* is the reason that you still are."

Nydia scowled, but she was still holding my hand.

"You're right," she said. "I do want this part. I don't want you to have this part because I want it. I didn't realise how much."

"If it's you," I told her, "I'll be really upset. I'll run off and I'll cry for about a day and a half, but then even though I'll still be jealous and fed up, I'll be glad for you. And I'll still be your friend who is proud and happy for you. Because, Nydia, you're my best friend and we're... well, we're like the Great Wall of China."

"What, you mean you can see us from outer space?" Nydia asked me, perplexed.

"No, I mean our friendship is strong with deep foundations and, most importantly, it's ancient. I wouldn't let anything come between us."

Nydia screwed her mouth into a sideways knot as she thought about what I'd said. "OK, perhaps I have been a bit unfair. Perhaps I should have let you explain about you and Sean, and maybe I didn't realise how badly I wanted the part of Arial. But I feel the same way as you do. If you get it I'll be upset. But I won't hate you. Because you are my best friend and you always have been and you always will be."

"Brilliant," I said, hugging her.

"It is a relief," Nydia said. "Because I'm rubbish at not being friends with you."

"Fancy a swim to cool off?" I asked her.

"Good idea," Nydia replied.

"Ahem," Mum stopped us as we were about to rush off. "Don't you want to know which one of you got the part?"

We both sat down with a bump and suddenly my heart was racing, thumping so hard that I thought I could hear it knocking against my ribcage.

"Christina said it was a very hard choice to make," Mum told us. "She said that all three of you girls were brilliant, but it was between you two. They weighed up everything they had seen in the auditions, and your film experience, Ruby, along with Nydia's experience of already playing the part. But in the end they said they chose the person who really embodied the essence of Arial, the person who lived with the same bravery and free spirit as she did."

And in that second I thought I knew who it was, but I was wrong.

Mum looked at Nydia and said, "I'm sorry, love." And then she looked at me and said, "Ruby, it's you."

teen girl! Magazine's

HOT PICKS

The hottest heat from the Hollywood Hills and beyond...

News, news, news!! This week at TGM! we can hardly move for all the top gossip that's landed on our desk, and true to you TGM! girls as always, we've been following up to find out what is fact and what is fiction.

FACT: We know what you want to know the most – **Sean Rivers** will be playing the lead role of Sebastian in ***Spotlight! The Movie Musical***. Our insider sources tell us that he hasn't signed a contract yet but that he has been heavily involved in the casting process. There's only one word that TGM! can use to describe this momentous news and it's "YESSS!"

FICTION: ***Hollywood High*** star **Adrienne Charles** has NOT been sacked from the show. Last week websites reported that the famously divatastic teen's contract had not been renewed as audience interest in her had started to plummet, but Blenheim Studios have confirmed that Adrienne is on board for the next two series and they are very happy to have her.

FACT: You heard it here first – in more ***Spotlight! The Movie Musical*** news, our very own Brit chick **Ruby Parker** has beaten ten squillion American girls to win the role of Arial opposite her old friend **Sean Rivers**! We've missed Ruby while she's been having her break from the limelight, nearly as much as we've missed Sean – and here at TGM! we reckon that Ruby and Sean have supported each other in this decision to take that step back into celebrity life. If you read this, guys, we're really glad you have!

FICTION: However TGM! can't find any truth to the rumour that Ruby and Sean are dating! As we know, Sean has been seeing model and actress **Mary-Anne Chase** for some time, but we hear that the sixteen-year-old has kissed that romance goodbye. Come on, Sean and Ruby, surely you must be more than JUST GOOD FRIENDS??????!!

FACT: Danny Harvey and ***Hollywood High*** hunk **Hunter Blake** are bezzie mates! I know – we're as shocked as you are! We thought that when the two brooding boys got together on the set of ***The Young Robin Hood***, they were bound to clash, but we have photographic evidence that they have been hanging out, playing football and getting on like a house on fire! Now there's a double date we'd like to go on with our BF!

FICTION: Rumour has it that **Danny Harvey** is spending a lot of time with another cast member, US teen telly star **Kirsty O'Brien**. You may not know her yet, but you wait until the release of *The Young Robin Hood* in the autumn. That girl's going places.

FACT: It's true – brave studio bosses have given famous boy rebel and eye-lined hottie **Henry Dufault** a role in *Spotlight! The Movie Musical.* We're really pleased; there's nothing we like more than the hard-living rock-and-roll type and Henry's certainly that – but will he stay the course or will he get himself kicked off this film too?

Keep watching this space for more news on the Ruby and Sean romance, Horrendous Henry, Spotlight! The Movie Musical, mean girl Adrienne Charles and much, much more...

Chapter Thirteen

I got the ripped-out pages of *Teen Girl! Magazine* a week later and scrawled across the bottom in thick black pen were the words, "Finally I get a mention and they don't even get my name right!!!!" It was Anne-Marie's (or Mary-Anne's) handwriting of course, but I knew that she had to be feeling a bit better otherwise she wouldn't have sent the article in the first place. With it came a letter describing how her holidays were going much better than she'd thought; her dad had delayed his next trip and stayed home for a whole week, even taking her out to buy a whole new wardrobe. She'd also bumped into the girls from Highgate Comp – Dakshima and Hannah and Talitha Penny in the park, and had been hanging out with them and flirting with the boys playing football. (She was careful at this point to tell Nydia that Gabe Martinez hadn't flirted at all and just looked a bit miserable because he was missing her.)

"I've even got quite friendly with Adele Adebayor,"

Anne-Marie wrote. "She's quite a laugh. I got her to walk past Jade Caruso and Menakshi Shah and look menacing. Maybe your school isn't so bad after all, Ruby. Anyway, miss you and Nydia loads – keep me posted on THE BIG DATE.

The big date was with Henry and it was happening that very night. It hadn't happened at any point in the previous week because the last seven days had been a tiny bit of a whirlwind.

After Mum had said I had been picked to play Arial, Nydia and I had looked at each other, not sure about what to say or do. There had been tears in Nydia's eyes and I felt really worried. But then she'd smiled and put her arms around me and hugged me really tightly.

"I love you, Ruby," she'd said with a shaky voice. "If it's not me, then I'm glad it's you. You deserve it."

"There's some good news for you too, Nydia," Mum said tentatively. "I know that Christina Darcy said you would only be considered for one role, but they were so impressed with you that they want you in the cast – in the role of Lena. It's not a main character, but she has a lot of scenes and—"

"A really big solo!" Nydia exclaimed. "'Dance Until Your Feet Bleed.' Lena gets the best song in the show – it's a huge dance number!"

"Exactly," Mum said. "Christina said she hoped you'd stick around over the summer and be part of the production and perform that song for them."

"Oh my God, that's amazing!" Nydia said.

"We're working together on a movie!" I said.

"A Hollywood movie!" she said.

And then we said something like, "ARRRRRRRRRRRRR-GHHHHHHHHHH!" Because we were really excited.

A few days later when I had slightly come down from cloud nine, to around cloud eight and a half, the date came up.

"So when *are* you going to go out with Henry?" Nydia asked me over breakfast.

"Henry Dufault?" Sean looked up, wide-eyed at the sound of that name. We had barely spoken two words to each other lately. I'd guessed that he'd seen his dad at least twice in the last week because he disappeared off, talking about meeting up with Danny. But he hadn't spent any time with me at all. He'd been pleased about the news and given me and Nydia a hug, but he'd kept his distance ever since. I wondered how we were going to get through a summer of preproduction rehearsals together – but then I remembered that whoever did play Sebastian to my Arial, it wasn't going to be Sean. And the fact that I knew that secretly made me cross.

"Yes, Henry Dufault," I said.

"Henry who?" Mum's head snapped up from the contract she was reading.

"*The* Henry Dufault?" Mrs Rivers asked me, in exactly the kind of tone that was bound to get a girl's mother anxious.

"Yes, that Henry," I said breezily. "He asked me if I'd like to go out for pizza with him sometime, that's all."

"Let me get this straight," Mum frowned. "We're talking about the same Henry Dufault who's just been given the part of Max in *Spotlight!* The boy who got thrown out of his last school for setting off the fire alarm twenty-seven times in one day?"

"He was going for a record..." I began before I realised that justifying some of Henry's bad behaviour was probably not the best plan if I really wanted to go on a date with him, even though up until this point I still hadn't really been sure about it. "Anyway, Mum, that stuff you read in the gossip magazines isn't real. Practically all of it is made up; you of all people should know that!"

"I don't think you should go on a date with Henry," Sean said.

"And what's it got to do with you?" I snapped back, making Nydia's eyes widen and the mums exchange glances.

"I'm just saying. Henry's a great kid, but he's trouble."

"Yes, well," I said stiffly. "At least he's honest. At least he says what he thinks and does what he says. At least he's not on the point of letting down hundreds and hundreds of people because of a stupid lie."

Sean held my gaze for a second longer, then dropped it.

"Who *is* going to do all of those horrible things?" Nydia asked.

"No one, no one," I said, looking away from Sean. "I'm just saying that at least Henry isn't going to do them."

"Oh," Nydia said, looking confused. "Right, well, that *is* good, I suppose."

"Perhaps Henry could come to tea," Mum suggested.

"Or perhaps we could go out for pizza like I said?" I countered. Up until this point I had been quite happy for there to be some unplanned date that Henry and I may or may not go on, but now that everyone was getting so flustered, I was determined to go.

"I don't know, Ruby," Mum said slowly. "All on your own in a big city in a foreign country with a boy I haven't met properly? I'm not sure."

"You'd let me go with Nydia and Sean," I protested.

"What a good idea," Mum said. "That's sorted then."

"What is? What's sorted?" I asked, getting the distinct

feeling that I'd just been outmanoeuvred by my mother.

"You can double date," Mum said. "You can take Nydia and Sean with you. I'd feel much better about it. I'll drive you to the pizza place and pick you up after. Now give me Henry's mother's number and I'll arrange it for tomorrow night."

"If I haven't died of mortification before then," I said, hanging my head in my hands as Nydia giggled.

"Sounds like a good idea to me," Sean said. Which meant it must be the worst idea in the history of the world EVER.

Henry texted me early next morning to tell me he was looking forward to our date. "Shame you have to bring half of LA too," he joked. At least I hoped he was joking. It was hard to tell with a text.

It took me and Nydia most of the afternoon to decide what I should wear. In the end I chose a pink cotton dress with a red cherry pattern on it. It took us about four hours to make it look casual, as if I had just slung it on at the last minute and didn't really care about how I looked at all.

It was nearly time to go and I was toying with putting on eyeshadow when Sean appeared in my open doorway, looking really gorgeous in a white shirt and jeans.

"You don't need make-up to look pretty," Sean said, noticing my finger hovering over a pot of light gold powder.

"I know," I said, patting some on my lids anyway, just to annoy him.

"You don't really like Henry, do you?" Sean said. "I mean, sure, he's an OK kid when you get to know him. Not nearly as crazy as the papers make out, but you don't like him the way you like me, do you?"

I turned around and looked at Sean. "He's uncomplicated... for a complicated person," I said. "He hasn't got a secret life with a secret dad that will get him into all sorts of trouble, and especially when his secret life comes out."

"I wish you'd stop doing that," Sean sighed. "I know I'm a mess. I really miss talking to you about it. You were the only person I could talk to." He looked a bit sad and anxious which made me feel a bit twisty in my tummy and worried for him.

"So, is it still going OK with your dad?" I asked him, my voice a bit softer. "You still think all of this is worth it?"

"Sort of," Sean said hesitantly. "Dad thinks that I've come so far in the process of playing Sebastian that I might as well go through with it now. He says it would be the best thing that I could ever do and that he'd manage me every step of the way. He says I'd be working for the rest of my life."

"Sean, you're sixteen years old. It seems a bit much to have your diary booked up until you're... oh, I don't know – seventy-eight!"

"That's kind of what I thought," Sean said. "But Dad really wants me to take the part."

"Do you think he wants that because it will be the best thing you can do for *you* or for *him*?" I asked. I knew Sean knew the answer, but I also knew that he wanted it to be different from what it was, and that sometimes you can want something so much that it's easier to believe it will happen than face the truth.

"I want to think that he wants what's best for me," Sean said. "And the funny thing is, since I've been back on set I *have* felt differently about acting again. After *The Lost Treasure of King Arthur* I never wanted to see another film set again. But I really like this film. I really like the script, the music and the other actors in it – some of them more than others." He smiled at me and I felt a lot of tiny little fireworks go off in my chest. "Maybe it wouldn't be so bad to go through with it."

"It would be *great* if you did the film," I told him warmly. "But only if that's what *you* want, not anybody else. You have to be sure that you'd be doing it for you. And you have to be sure soon, because your mum's had your contract for a few days now and as soon as she's had it checked by her lawyers, you'll be signed up and it will be much harder for everyone when you leave."

"I know," Sean said. "I'm going to work it out, Ruby. One way or another."

We stood there looking at each other for quite a long time until I heard my mum shouting up the stairs that it was time to go.

"You look really pretty," Sean said with a sad smile.

I couldn't help but feel as if I were walking on air as I went down the steps to meet Mum. It really was horribly inconvenient being in love with Sean Rivers.

Chapter Fourteen

"Hey, Ruby, hey, everyone." Henry was already at the pizza place when Mum dropped us off. He looked really nice, in a red shirt over black jeans and his cowboy boots.

"Hey, Henry," Sean said, with half a smile.

"Hi!" Nydia beamed.

"Hello, young man," my mum said. It turned out that she'd decided to follow us in. "I'll be back at 10.30 to pick you all up. Ruby, you have my number so call me if you need me to come sooner." She did her best motherly frown at Sean and Henry. "I'm depending on you boys to keep these girls safe, OK?"

"Yes, Mrs Parker," Sean said.

"I'll give it my best shot," Henry said, winking at me which made me laugh.

Mum didn't laugh though. "Hmmm," was the last thing she said before she went. And as it turned out she was right to be worried.

The pizza place was called Bella Fortuna and it

was really more of an Italian restaurant, but it was famous for serving the best pizzas for miles around. The waitress sat us at a round table in the centre of the restaurant and made a big deal about treating us as adults. It was really nice of her to make the effort, but it was quite embarrassing too and none of us really knew what to say. But things improved when our pizzas arrived. Food usually makes things better, I find.

"So, Ruby, what bands do you like?" Henry asked just as I took a huge bite out of my pepperoni feast.

"Bands?" I was taken aback. I liked music, but I had been so busy recently that I hadn't really heard of anyone cool or new. I was a rubbish teenager; most of my life was taken up with choir practice or rehearsal. I could tell him my top five musical numbers of all time, but when it came to bands, I realised that I was officially uncool.

"I like... all sorts of music really," I said. "What about you?" Henry reeled off the names of three or four bands that I'd never heard of, but I nodded along and occasionally said, "Oh, yeah, they are cool."

Henry leant back in his chair and sort of half smiled at me. I wondered if he knew that I was just pretending to know these bands and that maybe he was making them up to catch me out.

"You should be in a band, Henry," Nydia said. "You look like a rock star."

"I was in one for a while, until I got sacked," Henry said. "The lead guitarist was jealous of me. I might start my own band after this film though – want to be in it, Ruby?"

"Oh, no thanks," I said. "I've got exams next year." Everyone laughed and I belatedly realised why.

"You're quite a geek, aren't you?" Henry said, grinning at me.

I tried to be offended, but he was smiling as he said it and I think he sort of meant it as a compliment.

"Finally you've realised," Nydia joked. "The thing that Ruby used to be most famous for was that she was really terrible at rebelling."

"I kinda like that," Henry told me. "You're not trying to fit in or please anyone. You're just you – and you are pretty cool, geek or not."

I found myself smiling at Henry. I realised that I hadn't been annoyed by him so far that evening and we'd been together for over an hour now. Maybe I could date him after all. Then I noticed Sean rolling his eyes across the table and looking moody.

"Thank you, Henry," I said to annoy Sean. "That's a nice thing to say."

"Plus you're way pretty," Henry said. I blushed and

looked down at my hands. "I'd have told you that even if your mom hadn't made you bring the chaperones," he grinned. "But really I'm kinda hoping you'll wind up being my girlfriend."

At that moment a bright light went off in our faces. For a split second I thought that it was my brain finally exploding from boy-related confusion, but then I realised that it was a photographer. Even though we'd chosen Bella Fortuna because it was out of the way and on a block that the paparazzi hardly ever stalk, there must have been one walking past who looked in, spotted Sean Rivers and took his chance. Not only that, he'd marched right up to us and shoved his camera in Sean's face.

"C'mon, Sean, gimme a smile," the man said. Two or three more flashes went off as we shielded our eyes with our hands and everyone else in the restaurant turned and stared at us.

"Leave us alone," Henry said, standing up. "You can't photograph a group of minors against their will. Keep this up and I'll call the cops."

The photographer hesitated, then shrugged and took more frames. "I said *back off!*" Henry yelled, pushing the man back so hard that he crashed into the food-laden table behind. It tipped right over, leaving him flat on his back with his legs in the air.

"Where's the manager?" I said, standing up. I couldn't see a single waiter or waitress to ask for help.

"Maybe the waiting staff called the papers for publicity," Henry said quickly. "We need to get out of here..."

And then I noticed another commotion outside. A crowd jostled at the plate-glass window and I realised that there was now an army of photographers outside. A bank of flashes went off in my face and I couldn't see anything.

"We can get out the back way," Nydia said. She grabbed hold of Sean who had frozen, looking like a deer trapped in the headlights. "Come on, Sean, quickly."

"Don't worry, son, I'm here." Mr Rivers appeared almost out of nowhere, from somewhere at the rear of the restaurant. It seemed strange, but everything was happening so quickly I didn't really have time to think about it.

"Dad!" Sean snapped into life, a look of relief on his face. "I'm so glad you're here. Get us out!"

"Now take a breath, son," Mr Rivers said, putting his arm around Sean. "The best way to deal with these guys is to give them what they want. Stand tall and give them one of your million-dollar smiles."

Henry, Nydia and I watched uncertainly as Pat Rivers

turned Sean in the direction of the photographers, igniting another barrage of flashes that made Sean wince and blink. As he stood there next to Sean, a fixed grin on his face, Pat Rivers began talking to the other people in the restaurant, who were staring with open mouths.

"Sean Rivers is back and I can confirm to you right now that my son will be playing Sebastian in *Spotlight! The Movie Musical*. Go tell your husbands, wives, children and friends! Tell the whole world that you heard it here first."

"Dad?" Sean looked confused and really upset, almost in tears.

"Keep smiling, son," Mr Rivers said.

"I don't want to..."

"The whole world is watching you, Sean." The fake warmth in Mr Rivers' voice had vanished and his words sounded like a threat.

"Get off him!" I found myself yelling.

"It's fine," Sean's dad ignored me. "What better way to announce your return to the press? This will be all over the papers and magazines in the morning. The Rivers boys standing side by side for the whole world to see!"

"What about Mom?" Sean pleaded. "She'll know that I've lied to her."

"It had to come out sooner or later, Sean," Mr Rivers said. "It was lucky I happened to be here."

"I said get off him," I yelled again, surprised by my own anger. I grabbed Sean's arms and tried to drag him away, but Mr Rivers was holding on tight. "Sean, come *on*!"

"I've had enough of this," Henry said steadily. "This is ruining my date."

And then he charged, ramming his head into the older man's stomach so that Mr Rivers released Sean and staggered backwards, collapsing into some chairs.

"To the kitchens!" Henry yelled at us as he picked himself up. "Run!"

We raced between the tables and out into the hot, garlicky kitchen, where all the staff were loitering as if someone had told them to stay out of the way.

"No way do you get a tip!" Henry bellowed at them as we ran out into the parking lot. He looked around. "We've got about five seconds before the paps work out where we are."

Then Henry clocked a vegetable delivery van with the words 'Greta's Gorgeous Greens' painted on the side, along with an assortment of dancing cartoon vegetables. Its back doors were wide open.

"Get in there!" Henry yelled.

"*There?*" Nydia looked dubious.

But then we heard the pounding of feet and yells of "This

way!" from the paparazzi. They would be on us in a second.

"Just do it!" I said. I took Sean's hand and hauled him into the back of the van, swinging the doors closed behind Henry, who leapt in after Nydia.

Henry put a finger to his lips to remind us all to be quiet and we sat and waited.

It felt like we were in the back of Greta's Gorgeous Greens' van for ages, listening to the baying photographers and trying not to move or make a sound. After a while we heard Sean's dad's voice.

"You can go home now; you've got the photos I promised," he said. "Don't worry, I'll make sure that there are plenty more Sean exclusives for you. You just make your editors run the story – Pat Rivers and son reunited again. Legendary Hollywood manager takes on his biggest star yet! You know the score."

"Oh, Sean," I whispered. He was sitting next to me on an upturned empty crate and I realised that I was still holding his hand. In fact he was clutching my fingers so tightly that it hurt a little bit. I didn't let go though.

"I told him yesterday that we were coming here," Sean said quietly. "He must have arranged this whole thing. And tomorrow the photos will be all over the papers and Mom will know that I've been lying all this time. Why would he do that to me? That's not what he promised at all."

"It did kind of ruin our date," Henry said, looking at my hand in Sean's.

"Thanks for getting us out of there, Henry," Nydia said. "I couldn't believe that you pushed that sleazeball over and then took out Mr Rivers!"

"All in a day's work," Henry grinned.

"You're going to be in huge trouble," I said. "You assaulted two adults."

Henry shrugged. "I don't think either of them are going to be keen to explain that they were harassing a bunch of kids – and besides I've been in a lot worse trouble than *that*!" Henry winked at me, and I gave him a small smile in return.

"So we'll wait here until it's all quiet outside and then we can slip out," Henry told us as if he'd done this sort of thing a million times, which for all I knew he might have. "And then we'll..."

But just as Henry spoke we heard the driver's door open and slam, then a second later the sound of its engine turning on.

"We're moving!" Nydia exclaimed as the van lurched off.

Henry looked thoughtful. "The question is, where are we going?"

Chapter Fifteen

As we sat in the van we tried to work out what to do.

"I should call my mum," I said, reaching into my bag for my phone. "Tell her to come and get us."

"But from where?" Henry asked. "We don't know where we're going."

"We could tell her the name on the side of the van. She could tell the police to come and find us."

"Which means more press and more publicity," Henry pointed out. "I think that's a bad idea." He glanced at Sean, who was sitting with his head bent low over his knees. He was crying, but he didn't want us to know, so we were very careful not to look at him.

"Look," Henry went on. "This is a local business making local deliveries. Chances are that in a few minutes it will pull over at another drop-off and we'll be able to get out. But be ready to run because when they find four kids in the back of their van, they're going to be surprised."

"I think Henry's right," I said. "We should wait until we get out. Then I'll call Mum."

"The only thing is," Nydia said, looking at her watch. "It's after nine now – exactly how late do vegetables get delivered?"

Half an hour went by without the van parking, but at least there was lots of stopping and starting, which Henry said was for lights and traffic and meant we were still in the city at least. Then all of that changed and it felt as if we were on a long straight road. A road that could easily be the highway and taking us to goodness knows where.

"I hear San Francisco's nice this time of year," Nydia said nervously.

"Or Vegas," I added.

"Just as long as these aren't Mafia grocers," Henry joked, but no one laughed.

Then I realised that something was different. Sean had let go of my hand. He was sitting up straight, wiping his face on the back of his sleeve.

"You OK?" I asked.

He nodded. "I'll talk to Mom tonight," he said. "I have to explain everything to her. She's going to be so hurt and angry – she's going to ask me why. And I don't know what to tell her. But I know I have to explain everything, before she reads it in the papers."

"Look, Sean, you don't have to tell us right now if you don't want to," Nydia said slowly, "but what *was* going on in there? Why did your dad turn up and start acting as if you were his... biggest client. I thought you hadn't seen him for a year?"

Sean looked at me and I shrugged. "It's all coming out now anyway," I said.

"I guess," Sean said. Slowly he began to tell Nydia and Henry the whole story.

"So you're just going to ditch the rest of us at the last minute?" Nydia said crossly when he'd finished. "Sean, how could you?"

"Nydia," I intervened, "Sean's been through a lot. Now's not the time to have a go at him."

"I know that," Nydia said. "If I'd known about this from the beginning – like you obviously did – then I'd have had a go at him ages ago. Sean, you know what we've been through to get these parts. Audition after audition – and half of what we were being tested for was how we acted with *you*. If you leave they'll have to start from scratch again. Not only will it cost a fortune, but we might not even get to keep our parts."

"I hadn't thought about that," I admitted, suddenly feeling suddenly a little sick. Then I looked at Sean's stricken face. "But none of this is Sean's fault. It's his dad's. His dad has trapped him."

"He truly has," Henry put in. "Your dad knows that if you pull out now it won't just be the other actors you let down, or the studio – it will be your fans. Millions of them are expecting you to be in the film of the decade. If you don't do this film your career will effectively be over. No other studio will ever touch you, your reputation will be shot and your fan base too. Looks like your dad knew exactly what he was doing from the start. Man, you must earn him a lot of money!"

Sean shook his head and for a second I thought he might cry again, but he sniffed and took a breath and said, "I thought that dads had to love you. I thought that even if parents split up or other stuff happened they have to put you first. But that's not true. It's not true for a lot of kids. It's not true for Anne-Marie or me. And the stupid thing is... the *really* stupid thing is that even now, even knowing all that, I still love *him*. I still wish he was the kind of dad I want."

"What will you do, Sean?" I asked, putting my hand over his.

Sean shrugged. "The honest truth is that right now I don't know."

"Wait," Henry whispered. The van had drawn to a

halt and the engine was turned off. Quickly Henry opened the back door just a millimetre.

"If we get locked in then we're finished," he said. And a moment later we heard the van's central locking system clunk. After a few more seconds, Henry peered though the minute gap in the back door and then slowly pushed it open.

"The coast is clear," he said. "Follow me."

One by one we crept out into the night keeping our heads low. It looked like we were in the countryside, on a farm or something, because it was pitch-black and all I could hear were crickets chirruping.

"All we need to do now," Henry whispered as we crouched on the far side of the van, "is work out where the heck we are."

"Correction." A shadowy figure loomed out of the darkness. "All you kids need to do now is explain to me what you are doing in my van and why I shouldn't call the police right now."

Luckily for us Greta Tartucci was not the head of the local Mafia. She was an organic vegetable farmer from San Marino who had happened to be making a last-minute delivery to Bella Fortuna when everything kicked off. So when we explained what had happened, she was pretty understanding.

"I heard all the shouting so I ran inside," she said. "I didn't realise I'd left the van doors open. I was probably trying to call the police to come and clear those paparazzi rats away when you kids made a run for it – although the restaurant owner wouldn't thank me. If that's the kind of person he is I won't be delivering my gorgeous greens to *him* again." She folded her arms and looked at us.

"You don't know how lucky you are that I'm not a psycho axe-murderer – you can't just get into the back of a complete stranger's van, you know. Anything could have happened to you."

"But we didn't plan to stay there," I explained. "We were going to get out again – but then you drove off."

"You should have banged on the partition," Greta said. "Got me to pull over. I would have driven you home."

"We didn't know if you were a psycho axe-murderer or not," Henry said.

"Or in the Mafia," Nydia added.

"Well, you need to call your parents, right now, before they go out of their minds with worry. Then you can pass them on to me and I'll give them directions to the farm."

I nodded and dialled Mum's number.

"Ruby!" Mum picked up on the first ring. "Where are you? I just arrived at the restaurant to pick you up and it's closed. Are you OK?"

"I'm fine, Mum," I said. "We all are. It's just that, well, we got a little bit lost..."

"So where are you?" Mum asked me.

"An organic vegetable farm in San Marino," I told her slowly. "Near Pasadena."

"Pasa—" But before Mum could say any more I handed the phone to Greta. There would be enough explaining to do later; I didn't feel like starting now.

"Aren't you going to ring your folks?" I asked Henry who was on his own in the living room looking out of the window at the moon, while Sean and Nydia sat at Greta's kitchen table.

"Nope," Henry said. "They're not expecting me back until later. I figure I'll get a lift home with your mom and go home from there. They won't have to worry about me any more than usual."

"They really don't expect you home until after midnight?" I said, looking at my watch.

"They've given up setting me a curfew," Henry explained. "I always used to break them, stay out all night, get into trouble. This way I usually get home at an OK time, in one piece, and everyone is happy."

"You have very laid-back parents," I told him. "My mum would kill me dead if I did that sort of thing."

"I don't rate your chances of surviving the night then," Henry smiled at me. "Actually my parents are just really, really tired. I've worn them out. So now they just stand back and do the best they can."

I frowned. "Why are you like that, Henry?" I asked. "Can't you just, you know, be normal sometimes? Why do you always have to break the rules?"

Henry tapped his finger on the window pane for a second and looked back out at the moon. "Attention deficit hyperactivity disorder," he said.

"Huh?"

"ADHD. I've had it since I was a kid – it's this thing, some messed up wiring in my head that means I go crazy with boredom every five seconds. It's really hard to concentrate or remember things – I say stuff that I know I shouldn't, but it comes out of my mouth anyway. And trouble seems to follow me around. I might grow out of it, but then I wouldn't be me any more. I don't really know who I would be. Do you know what I mean?"

"I think so," I said, trying to take it in. I'd never actually known anyone with a condition before, unless you counted Jade Caruso's dandruff problem. I was trying to work out if I should feel less annoyed with him now that I knew he had ADHD, or if I should be scared. After all, exactly how mental was he?

And then I realised I was being stupid. He was still the same Henry now that he'd been five minutes ago, only he'd trusted me with the truth. Yes, he was a bit hard to take sometimes, but there was something about him I really liked. The bit that said what he felt and did what he liked; the bit that I didn't have.

"They gave me these pills when I was little," Henry told me. "But all they did was zombify me and make me feel down all the time. I'm lucky I guess that Mom and Dad didn't want that for me either. They looked into alternative therapies, breathing exercises, changed my diet and stuff. I exercise a real lot and a couple of years ago I got into music and acting, and those things seem to keep me on track for longer than thirty seconds. And I'm doing pretty well actually. I'm pretty happy, even if sometimes I just wonder what would happen if I set off twenty-seven fire alarms in one afternoon." He grinned at me. "Anyway you don't have to worry. Most of the time I'm pretty normal, with a few exceptions."

"Like what?" I asked him.

"Like when I'm overtired and I go really fruit loops, or like when I'm standing next to a really pretty girl that I want to kiss."

"Really, what do you do when that... oh, you mean me."

"Yes, I do," Henry said. "And if I don't kiss you now anything could happen."

I glanced back into the other room where Sean was still sitting with Nydia and Greta, and then I thought – well, why not? So I leant over and kissed Henry before he could kiss me. It was a nice kiss, sweet and not scary. And I really hoped that I'd get butterflies or fireworks or any of the things that I got whenever I was around Sean these days. But I didn't.

"So, Ruby," Henry said as we looked at each other. "Before we get carted off home, can I ask you something?"

"Are you going to ask me to be your girlfriend?" I said.

Henry blinked. "Well, yeah, it was kinda going to be that."

"Henry, I really, really like you," I said. "And this has nothing to do with ADHD, but I can't be your girlfriend."

"It's because of your giant crush on Sean Rivers, isn't it?" Henry asked me bluntly.

"Is it that obvious?" I asked him.

"You might as well write it on your forehead," Henry said. "So if you like him and he likes you, why *aren't* you his girlfriend?"

"Because he was going out with my best friend," I explained.

"Ah – it's the whole girls' honour code," Henry nodded. "I never did get that. Anyway, in the mean time, you should know that I am very available to take you for dates and there's a roughly ten per cent chance that all of them will end in total disaster."

I smiled at him and said, "Henry Dufault, you are not nearly as bad as you make out."

"Don't you believe it, babe," Henry said.

Then we heard a knock at the door and walked into the other room as Greta went to open it.

"Ruby Parker!" My mum marched into the room, followed closely by Sean's mum, who was holding an early edition of the morning papers. "What on *earth* is going on?"

TEEN SENSATION SEAN RIVERS BOUNCES BACK WITH A BANG!

This reporter can confirm that as of last night former teen star Sean Rivers will be back on the big screen this fall in the year's most talked-about film, *Spotlight! The Movie Musical!*

BREAKDOWN!

Sean, now 16, gave up the limelight after a very public break up with his father and one-time manager, Beverly Hills legend Pat Rivers. Sean was reunited with his estranged mother and lived quietly in England where he attended a stage school and lived as normal a life as such a famous boy could.

SHOCKING!

And yet only twelve months later Sean is back working with his father again, in a move that Pat Rivers has welcomed. Rivers' management company took a huge hit after Sean revealed how hard his father made his life. Mr Rivers said of the reconciliation: "It's the proudest and happiest moment of my life to have my son back again. We're closer than ever and I know I can guide him to the career heights that a boy of his talent deserves."

HYSTERIA!

Girls around the world wept when Sean retired from acting and there has been an almost equal amount of hysteria online since the photos shown here (top right) were posted on the Internet last night. There are already several fansites welcoming Sean back and expressing encouragement and support for his brave return. Will Sean Rivers still have the same magic that made the whole world love him? We'll have to wait and see.

Chapter Sixteen

The following day Nydia and I were sitting by Jeremy's pool waiting. We still had no idea what Sean planned to do about the film which meant that we still had no idea what was going to happen to us.

As it turned out we stayed at Greta Tartucci's farm for so long that my mum insisted on calling Henry's mother and explaining where he was whether Henry thought it necessary or not. Mum said that Mrs Dufault was really glad to know where he was and wasn't quite as cool about him being out all hours as Henry liked to make out. But anyway Greta had made toast and tea and we explained what had happened. Not just on that night, but over the last few weeks. Sean sat his mum down and told her everything.

I watched her face as she listened to Sean. At first she was shocked, then there was anger and then finally, as he explained how his dad had set him up in Bella Fortuna, it was sadness. Two big fat tears rolled down her cheeks and she looked really hurt, not for herself but for Sean.

"Why didn't you tell me you were missing your father, Sean?" she asked him softly. Sean looked uncomfortable as he tried to work out what to say. I wished that I could give him a hug, but I knew I couldn't so I twisted my fingers together, as I watched him tying his own into worried knots.

"Because... you hate him," he said finally. "You're always saying how much you hate him. I didn't think you'd let me see him."

"I wouldn't have stopped you," Sean's mum said. "I would have protected you from... from all of this!" She gestured at the open paper that had already run a story on Sean, including the photos that were taken earlier that evening. "Honey, I would have stopped you getting yourself into this mess. Don't you trust me?"

"I'm sorry, Mom," Sean said. "I do trust you – I got confused... I'm sorry."

His mum reached out and put an arm around him. "Don't be sorry," she said, kissing the top of his head. "What's done is done and now you've got me on your side. We'll figure this out one way or another, don't you worry."

"And you've got us too," I reminded him.

"We'll stick by you whatever happens," Nydia said. "As soon as you've decided what you're going to do."

"So you didn't ever really want to come back to the movies?" Sean's mum asked him. "And taking the part of Sebastian was a front to stick around in Hollywood?"

Sean nodded. "I feel like such an idiot."

"Honey, I don't want you to worry about anything," his mum told him. "Don't worry about the studio, the contract or even your fans. The only thing that matters is you and if you're not ready for this then you just won't do it. It's as simple as that. I'll have you back in London within twenty-four hours and you'll be kicking a ball in the park with your mates before you know it."

"I know," Sean said. "I need some time to think about everything that's happened and... I need to talk to Dad again."

"Really?" Sean's mum looked shocked. "After everything he's done."

"Yes," Sean insisted. "*Because* of everything he's done. I need to talk to him – to see if there's even a bit of him that cares about me, about the boy that's his son and not Sean Rivers movie star. So will you call him and ask him to come over tomorrow?"

"If that's what you want," Sean's mum said dubiously.

"And after I've spoken to him," Sean said, looking at me, "that's when I'll know what to do."

Nydia and I had tried to sleep when we got back, but we couldn't. She had sneaked into my room and we lay awake almost all night talking about everything that had happened and what it might mean.

"Maybe this isn't our big break after all," Nydia said. "Maybe this time next week we'll all be in London again with the rest of the boring holidays to get through."

"Maybe," I sighed. "But on the bright side you'd see a lot more of Gabe."

"I like Gabe a lot," Nydia said, "but at the end of the day, he's just a boy. This is my career we're talking about."

"There'll be other big chances," I said, turning to look at her in the darkness.

"Will there?" Nydia asked me. "How many big chances does a person get? Think about how many actors and actresses there are in the world. Millions and millions. And how many are famous or even get regular work? Hardly any. Everyone's waiting for their big break and this was mine." She looked out of the window where the city lights still burned below us in the valley. "I know that if Sean pulls out of the film it's what he has to do.

But if he does then it will probably be over for us too."

"It might not be," I said. "If any role is likely to get recast it's mine, not yours. Come on – chin up, you're usually such an optimist."

"That was until I came to Hollywood," Nydia said. "It's dog eat dog out here."

"Except for David because he wouldn't fill anyone up," I said, patting the tiny dog on his scrawny head.

"So what happened between you and Henry?" Nydia asked me on a big long yawn. I told her about the kiss and him asking me out, but not about the ADHD. I thought that was up to him to tell her if he wanted to.

"But you're not going to go out with him again?" Nydia asked me.

I shook my head. "I suppose I could and it would be fun and everything, but... It sounds silly, but my heart's not in it."

"You really like Sean, don't you?" Nydia peered at me in the gloom. I shrugged. "Go on, you can tell me. I won't throw a strop."

"I do a bit," I said, by which I mean a massively large amount.

"And he really likes you, the idiot," Nydia said.

"Yes, but neither of us wants to hurt Anne-Marie," I said quickly.

“I know you don’t, now,” Nydia said. “Although the way she found out could have been handled a lot better. Look, Annie’s hurting now, but she won’t feel that way forever. She’ll be happy again really soon and then I bet she won’t mind about you and Sean at all. You just have to wait.”

“Really?” I said uncertainly. “Do you think so?”

“Yes, I do,” Nydia said. “Why does that seem to scare you.”

“Because it’s Sean. *Sean Rivers*. Imagine me, Ruby Parker, being Sean Rivers’ girlfriend. That is crazy!”

“You can say that again!” Nydia had laughed and we’d talked some more, until at some point just before dawn we’d drifted off to sleep.

As we waited by the pool Mum came out to join us with some juice and pancakes. “I’ve had your rehearsal schedule faxed through from the studio,” she said, sitting on the end of one of the sunloungers.

“Assuming all goes to plan, you’ll be rehearsing for the whole of the summer break and begin shooting in September, so obviously you won’t be able to go back to school in London. But the studio will set up a school on set for all the students. Remember Fran Francisco?” she asked me. "She taught you while you were working on *The Lost Treasure of King Arthur.* Well, she'll be teaching you again. We'll be living over here for the next four months until Christmas."

"That's ages. We'd probably get really bored and homesick after a while," Nydia said.

"And on set, school isn't nearly as much fun as it sounds," I said. "That Fran Francisco is nearly as strict as Ms Lighthouse!"

"Plus imagine having to spend the whole summer learning cool dance moves and singing great songs," Nydia added wistfully.

"It would be awful," I said. "I actually hope that Sean wants to go home. I actually think that that would be best all round."

"You're doing a good job of keeping your chins up, girls," Mum said. "Pat Rivers will be here soon. Why don't you go and have a shower and get dressed. It's always better to face your fate with a clean face."

"OK, Mum," I said, looking at Nydia. "After all we've been taught by Sylvia Lighthouse. We know all about keeping our chins up, come what may."

I was washed and dressed and on my way downstairs

when I noticed Sean's bedroom door was open. He was sitting on the edge of his bed, his hands gripping the sides as if he were afraid he might fall off. His dad was due to arrive any minute.

"Are you OK?" I asked him, standing in the doorway.

He looked up at me and smiled. "Come and sit next to me for a bit," he said. After a second's hesitation I did, deciding it couldn't hurt. I liked sitting next to him.

"Ruby," he said, "I just want to thank you. You've been a really great friend to me since we got here."

"Been?" I half laughed. "That sounds sort of ominous. That sounds sort of like you're not going to be my friend soon."

"No, that's not what I mean. I mean I've messed things up a lot by telling you how I feel. I've made life really difficult for you and I'm sorry. I don't know what I'd do without you as my friend."

"Well, you won't have to know," I said, getting a bit annoyed by all this talk of "friends". Was Sean trying to tell me that he'd gone off me?

"Good." Sean looked at me, slid his right hand over my left and leant towards me. "You're the coolest girl I know, Ruby Parker," he said, his lips very close to mine. I got the distinct feeling that I didn't have to worry after all.

"I've always thought so," I squeaked.

"Do you remember when I had to kiss you in the audition, and I said you didn't have to worry because it was Sebastian kissing you and not me?"

I nodded, deciding that talking wasn't my best thing just then.

"Well, start worrying, because now it's me who's going to kiss you."

And when Sean kissed me there were fireworks, butterflies, an army of fizz pops and a whole host of goosebumps.

I think he'd probably stopped kissing me for two or three seconds before I finally opened my eyes.

"Now," Sean said with his old grin, "I know that I can face my dad."

"Good," I managed to say. "That's good." And I was secretly thinking that was lucky because right now I didn't think my knees would ever work again.

Downstairs we heard the doorbell go and David launch into a yapping frenzy.

"He's here," Sean said, standing up.

"You'll be brilliant," I told him.

He nodded. "I will. And thanks to you I know exactly what to do."

* * *

Sean had asked us all to be there when he saw his dad. Pat Rivers looked at us sitting around Jeremy's living room as if we were the enemy, which I suppose we were really. We'd all certainly have really liked to punch him if we had been the sort of people to condone violence, which we weren't. Although I rather wished that Henry was there to do another flying tackle.

"So your mother's stuck her oar in then?" Mr Rivers sneered, nodding in the direction of Sean's mum.

"She's made me realise I shouldn't have been seeing you in secret," Sean said stiffly. He was locking all of his feelings inside, but I could see the tension in his face.

"Look, son, I know the way things came out wasn't exactly how you would have chosen, but you've been away so long. You needed to come back with real impact. You had to wake this town up, make it sit up and pay attention to Sean Rivers."

"But, Dad," Sean kept his voice level. "I wasn't coming back. You know that. I was never going to actually make the movie. I only did it so I could spend some more time with you. The whole thing was your idea."

"I know that's how you felt to begin with," Mr Rivers said, giving a very good impression of a man who cared. "But I knew that once you were back on the lot you'd get that old feeling back. You'd really want to be part of something as special as this movie. I knew that in the end I'd get you to see reason." Mr Rivers took a step closer to Sean. "Look, son, your mother wants to hold you back; she always has, wanting this so-called 'normal' life for you. But you wouldn't be happy with a normal life – and you know that I'm right. If I was wrong then why else would you have come to find me?"

"Because I love you, Dad," Sean said. "And I wanted you in my life. Not because I wanted you to manage my career. I just wanted a dad."

"But don't you see? I can do both!" Mr Rivers promised. "As your manager I can be your dad and control... I mean build your career."

"Dad..." Sean paused and looked at me. "I've decided. I'm not going to do *Spotlight!*—"

"What?" Mr River shouted at him, making us all jump. "You are going to throw away this opportunity – are you crazy? Do you realise how much money I – *we* could make from this movie, the record deal, merchandising? It's a bottomless pit of cash. This deal would set us up for life, Sean. And you're walking away from it because you're a wimp, a pathetic, no good, waste of space wimp – and you're no son of mine."

I gasped and looked at Sean, expecting him to crumple, but all he did was smile.

"Dad, you didn't let me finish," he said calmly. "What I was about to say was that I'm not going to do *Spotlight!* with you as my manager. Or actually with you involved in my life at all. But I *am* going to do the film. You were right about one thing. When I got back on set, I realised how much I missed the buzz and how brilliant movie people can be to work with. People who care about the film and each other. I've loved every second of it and now I know that I'm ready to work again – but not with you anywhere near me. So when you see the CD in the shops, or the doll advertised in store windows or the DVD spending weeks at number one, then you'll know that you aren't going to make another single cent out of me ever again."

"Why, you...!"

I shrieked as Pat Rivers rushed at Sean, and I was sure he was about to hit him, when something wonderful happened.

"THAT IS QUITE ENOUGH!" A loud male voice stopped him in his tracks. I have never been so relieved to see my dad standing in the doorway, even looking quite tough and macho for once, despite his bald patch.

"Don't you lay a finger on that boy," Dad told Mr Rivers in his best telling-off voice. "Otherwise you'll have me to deal with."

"I'll sue," Mr Rivers said.

"For what?" Sean said. "I never signed anything, and even if I did it wouldn't count unless Mom had signed it too. Your plan failed, Dad. You lost."

"But you're my son. You belong to me."

"No, I don't," Sean said simply. "I am not your son any more. Goodbye, Dad."

Finally Mr Rivers turned on his heel, pushed his way past Dad and made his way out, chased by a furious David yapping at his heels.

"Dad!" I said, running into his arms. "I'm so glad to see you!"

"Well, I couldn't let all this excitement go on without me," Dad said, looking very pleased with himself. "I thought it was time for a surprise visit."

"And Sean!" I looked at him and my eyes filled with tears. "You were so amazing!"

"You were incredible," Sean's mum agreed. "I am so proud of you, my strong, brave son."

"You were pretty cool," Nydia agreed, patting Sean on the back.

"Well," Mum said, coming over to hug me and Dad. "Looks like it's all systems go for *Spotlight! The Movie Musical*."

"And you know what that means," I said to Sean and Nydia. "This isn't the end at all. It's just the beginning!"

What's in the stars for Ruby Parker?

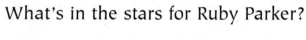

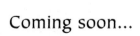

Find out in

Ruby Parker

SuperStar!

Coming soon...